THE TUNNELS

(A HARBOR SECRET - BOOK 1)

The Tunnels © 2016 Kristie L. Dickinson

All rights reserved

Amazon Kindle Edition, License Notes

This ebook is licensed for your personal enjoyment only. This ebook may not be re-sold or given away to other people. If you would like to share this book with another person, please purchase an additional copy for each recipient. If you would like to share this book with another person, please purchase an additional copy for each recipient. If you're reading this book and did not purchase it or it was not purchased for your use only, then please purchase your own copy. The ebook contained herein constitutes a copyrighted work and may not be reproduced, transmitted, downloaded, or stored in or introduced into an information storage and retrieval system in any form or by any means, whether electronic or mechanical, now known or hereinafter invented, without the express written permission of the copyright owner, except in the case of brief quotation embodied in the critical articles and reviews. Thank you for respecting the hard work of this author.

This ebook is a work of fiction. The names, characters, places, and incidents are products of the writer's imagination or have been used fictitiously and are not to be construed as real. Any resemblance to persons, living or dead, actual events, locales, or organizations is entirely coincidental.

Edited by Cassandra Heos

Cover by Sheri McGathy

Special thanks to Richard Wiles

Thanks to Ted O'Dell

Author photo by Maya Murshak Parks

To Cookie and Cupcake, my foster puppies. I hope you are living happily ever after.

The Tunnels

Prologue

"She'll never give you the time of day, so you might as well stop staring at her," the bartender advised Maitre d' Paul Preston as he wiped down the bar on one of the busiest nights Club Manitou had seen.

Paul took a slow draw on his cigarette and smiled confidently before exhaling. He looked back across the room again at the woman sipping liquor out of a tea cup, just as they all did in case of a raid. She set the cup down and used her thumb to remove the red lipstick mark left on it, using the distraction to throw him a sideways glance.

The bartender stopped wiping and leaned his elbows on the bar across from Paul, effectively mirroring him. "Even if she wasn't married, the likes of her would never become involved with the likes of you."

The maître d' exhaled and moved his gaze from the beautiful sipper to the bartender. "And what makes you say that,

Scotty?"

The bartender leaned in closer and pressed a finger against the side of his nose. "Because you're crooked, and she comes from some hoity-toity Detroit family."

Paul smirked and looked back at the woman with wavy, short brown hair as he continued to talk. "Crooked is just a matter of perspective, Scotty."

Scotty let out a snort. "They don't get much more crooked than The Purple Gang."

Still smirking with confidence, Paul made eye contact when the woman glanced at him again. He leaned in to the bartender as he put out his cigarette in an ashtray on the bar. "As I said, Scotty, it's all a matter of perspective."

He stepped away from the bartender, passed the large double-sided fireplace that separated the basement bar and lounge from the game room, and crossed to the wait station. Standing close to the rest room doors, he kept his head down as he pretended to check the wait station over, unnecessarily moving a creamer pot and checking the sugars.

He felt her approaching before he turned to see her hesitate purposefully before stepping into the ladies room. Glancing around to be sure everyone was otherwise occupied, he stepped in behind her and locked the door.

"We've got to stop meeting like – "

Before he could finish, her arms were wrapped around him, her red lipstick leaving its mark on his mouth. His hands moved into the waves of her short, brown hair, and for a moment the realities of their lives disappeared as they stole time that didn't belong to either one of them.

Minutes ticked by as the two began to consummate their affair when a gunshot exploded.

"What was that?" Phyllis asked, pulling back.

The gunshot was followed by a heavy rolling sound. "They've closed the steel door at the base of the stairs," he informed. "It's a raid." He pulled away from her and started to tuck his shirt in.

"A raid?" Phyllis looked panicked. "So we're trapped down here?"

Paul looked around with calm eyes. The plan he'd been over a hundred times with the staff would be going into effect any second now, but his mind was instead on an opportunity. His focus left the surroundings and returned to her. "This is our chance, Phyllis."

"Chance?"

"We can get out of here and start fresh." Phyllis looked stunned, and he expounded. "We can get out of here, move far, far away, and start a life together." His hands moved to her shoulders now as his spontaneous plan became clear to him. "A life where no one knows who we are or where we came from."

"Just disappear?" She looked around the bathroom, confused.

He heard the noise of liquor bottles clinking as they were packed into crates just outside the door. "We have to go now. Are you with me?"

She searched his eyes, wondering if she could believe him. She had a comfortable life as the only daughter to the prestigious Whitley family of Detroit. Her eyes wandered as she also remembered the much-older husband she would be giving up. The husband who had indiscreet affairs. He was a husband who had been friends with her father, and she had been awarded to him like nothing more than a chip in a poker game.

Her brown eyes met his. "Yes," she said with certainty.

Paul unlocked the door for his staff before moving in a few steps to the back wall of the rest room. Reaching behind an overlapping seam of the wallpaper, she saw him push into the wall before stepping back to effortlessly pull a cement-block door open whose hinges were hidden behind another seam of loose wallpaper. Behind the door was a room stocked to the ceiling with bottles of liquor on the front wall. Lining the back wall were floor-to-ceiling shelves of poker chips and decks of playing cards.

"We're hiding in there?"

"No." He put an arm protectively on her low back, guiding

her into the hidden room before pulling the concrete door closed behind him.

She heard two bullets fired followed by the sound of them ricocheting off of the eight-inch-thick steel door that had been rolled across the entrance to the basement.

Moving with lightning speed, Paul removed two shelves of poker chips against the back wall and set them conveniently on the only two empty shelves. He pushed on the wall behind the remaining shelves, and Phyllis saw that it was, in fact, another door. What appeared before her was a large tunnel lined with square cobblestones around its entire circumference.

Phyllis gasped before leaning forward to peer into the tunnel. "It must be six feet high," she mumbled more to herself than to Paul. Her eyes strained to see the exit, but she could only make out roots that snuck through the ceiling pavers and hung into the dark hole that looked like it went straight to hell. "I can't go in there."

Knowing the staff would be bringing the liquor on the floor

in to safely stash during the raid, Paul held out his arm, urging her into the tunnel. "Do you trust me?"

She looked into his eyes again, knowing there was no going back to her old life if she followed him.

There were yells and loud thuds against the steel door now as the authorities tried to gain entrance to the basement. Screams and chaos were outside the door that secluded the two secret lovers. Paul heard his staff in the rest room now, attempting to open the concrete door he and Phyllis had just stepped through.

"Do you trust me?" he repeated.

With both fear and shock in her dark eyes, she nodded. "Yes, I trust you."

He gestured again, and she ducked through the opening made by the two removed shelves and into the tunnel that would change her life. Paul closed the door behind them as Phyllis heard his staff step into the hidden room.

CHAPTER 1

"Cupcake!" Kylie called in panic. She looked frantically from side to side through the thick hardwood forest as dusk set in. "Cupcakie, where are you?" She ran further along the path in the forest. She and her rescue puppy had only been living in the old house for a week. Every evening after work, they had gone running on a footpath through the forest surrounding the house. At first, she had kept Cupcake on a leash. The last two nights, she had let the pit-mix puppy run off leash so she could stretch her legs. Tonight she had disappeared.

"Cupcake, come!" she commanded, hoping the puppy would remember something from their obedience class. She paused her run to listen, her heart thumping. A bird screeched in the distance. A branch snapped to Kylie's left, and she spun to follow the sound with her eyes, but she saw nothing.

She grabbed the earbuds hanging at her waist and coiled them as she turned to start walking back to the house. Her eyes were wide as she looked side to side in the eerie forest. "Cupcake, you come back right now!" she called again, her voice cracking at the end of the command as emotion overtook her.

The longer she walked along the path, the darker it grew. Paranoia set in as the sounds of the night filled in around her. The sweat from her run grew cold, and she decided to start a slow jog again to keep warm. "Cupcake!" she called again. This time she thought she heard something and stopped her run. Her eyes large as she looked into the deep dusk, she called her dog again, this time with a question in her call. "Cupcake?"

She stood and held her breath as she listened for a response. Her head snapped to the left as she heard the whimper again. "Cupcake!" She ran off the path towards the sound and into the dusky forest. After a hundred yards, she slowed her pace and, after two hundred yards, she stopped again. "Cupcakie, where are you?" She stood still and listened. Seconds ticked by before she heard a little yip.

Her eyes followed the sound. "Cupcake?" She moved cautiously towards the sound, not seeing her dog. She stopped and listened again. It was only moments before she heard the familiar thudding of her puppy's tail. Even though she didn't see the dog, a wave of relief swept over her. "Cupcakie?" she whispered before she stepped and felt air beneath her foot. Catching herself, she fell to her right and onto her side, hitting her shoulder hard on the ground. An "Oof" escaped her lips.

She propped herself up on her elbow and squinted her eyes as she looked at the hole in front of her. Inching to the edge, she looked down into the dark pit and saw Cupcake sitting at the bottom, her tail thumping out her happiness.

Relieved to have found the dog, tears welled in Kylie's eyes as she looked down the hole that must have been twelve feet deep. "Oh, Cupcake, are you okay?"

The dog smiled up at its owner.

"Oh, baby, let mommy figure something out." She pushed back and looked around for something to fish her dog out of the pit with. Seeing nothing, she dug her cell phone out of the pocket of her running pants. She dialed the 9-1 part of 9-1-1 and then stopped. Was this a 9-1-1 emergency? Wasn't that reserved for fires, heart attacks, and wars?

She looked around at the quickly impending darkness, scrolled through her contact list, and dialed a different number instead.

"Hello?"

"Chief Lange?"

"Yeah."

She let out a sigh of relief. "This is Kylie from the cupcake shop."

"Hi, Kylie from the cupcake shop," he flirted with her.

She rolled her eyes. She didn't have time for this. "Look, my dog fell in some sort of hole in the woods while we were out running." She tried to hold back the panic in her throat. "It's getting dark, and I don't know what to do."

"So you called me?"

"You're the fire chief. I didn't know if I should call 9-1-1."

The flirty tone in his voice evaporated as the seriousness of the situation set in. "Will a ladder fit into the pit?"

Kylie eyed the dark hole. "I think so."

"Where are you?"

"Down one of the footpaths behind the old Gerhart place."

"The Gerhart place?"

"Just hurry," Kylie cut him off. "It's almost dark."

A rustling sound on the other end of the phone indicated the man was gathering things as he spoke on the phone. "I'm on my way. I'll call you when I'm in the parking lot, and you can tell me which way to go."

Despite the desperate situation, Kylie felt a small wave of relief as she heard his car start. "Okay." She paused a moment before following up with a weak, "Thanks."

She felt every minute tick by painfully slowly as she lay on her side next to the hole, whispering words of comfort to her puppy below. As it became completely dark, she heard the night sounds of the forest all around her. An occasional stick snapped, leaves rustled, what she hoped was a bird screeched, and a million hidden eyes stared at her as she lay in the dark.

She'd only owned the abandoned building for a week now. Built in the 1920s, it had once been a popular speakeasy in northern Michigan, but the end of prohibition and a fire had put the place out of commission. With stars in her eyes and visions of a Christmas tree and a family in the home someday, she'd made an impulse buy and gotten the home for a steal. For now, the only family would have to be Kylie and Cupcake, provided Cupcake made it out of her predicament in one piece.

Her stomach was in a tight knot by the time her cell phone finally rang. "Are you there?" she asked in panic, skipping the greeting.

"Where are you?" he asked back.

She swallowed, trying to remain calm. "There's a footpath that goes off the back of the parking lot."

Only a few seconds ticked by before she heard, "Okay, I'm on it."

"Go until you have the option to take a left."

Minutes ticked by as she heard the firefighter breathing heavily as he carried his ladder and gear down the footpath. Completely distracted by the phone call, she was startled to hear the leaves rustle loudly near her. Sweat broke out on her chest. "Shoo!"

"What?"

"Go away!"

"What?"

Her eyes were wide as she yelled more loudly, "Go away!"

"Are you okay?"

Her voice cracked as she whispered back, "Just hurry,

please." She looked into the darkness with searching eyes again. "Something else is out here."

There was another rustle near her. "Oh, God!" she panicked loudly in both fear and an effort to scare the rustler.

"Do I just stay on this path?"

Drawing her attention back to the phone, she said loudly, "Yes. It will circle around the house and then turn sharply to the right. I'll watch for your light." She turned back to where the rustling sound had come from and said loudly, "Someone's coming. They'll be here any minute."

She heard a stick snap under heavy weight and considered jumping into the pit with Cupcake for safety. "Cupcake, you are never running off leash in the woods again, do you hear me?" she scolded into the hole.

The puppy let out a soft whimper from the dark hole.

"Do you see my light yet?" she heard on the phone.

She lifted her head and looked through the black forest.

"No, not yet."

"How far did you run anyway?"

She shrugged. "I had to wear off three cupcakes."

"Do you see my light now?"

"No. Are you walking or running?"

There was a pause on the phone. "Trotting."

She started to smile when she heard another rustling sound, this time closer. She stayed laying down and closed her eyes, waiting for her fate to overcome her.

"Chief, there's something making noise nearby," she whispered in a frightened voice.

She heard him panting now. "Heavy noise or soft noise?"

"Heavy."

"Do you smell anything?"

"What?"

"Do you smell something?"

Kylie inhaled purposefully before responding. "No."

"Good."

"Why?"

"If it was a bear, you'd smell it."

Panic overcame her as she sat up. "A bear? There are bears here?"

He hesitated before responding, not wanting to scare her. "Not many."

Kylie swallowed hard and stared into the darkness. "I think I see you."

"I can only hope. Geez, how far did you go?"

She relaxed a little again. "I told you, I'm a big eater." She saw the light draw nearer on the path. "Okay, now turn to your right." The light pointed towards her. "We're about two hundred yards ahead."

As the light moved towards her, she cautioned, "Be careful. I don't know if there are other holes around."

The light didn't heed her warning and kept progressing at a rapid pace. "Kylie, where are you?"

She hung up her phone and stood. "Over here."

Through the darkness came the local fire chief with a ladder, flashlight, and a head lamp. "Are you okay?"

Her fear turned to relief, and she wrapped her arms up and around his broad shoulders, eager for his protection from whatever had been making the sounds nearby. "Thank you. Thank you for coming." She dropped her forehead against his shoulder. "I didn't know who else to call."

He embraced her back, speaking softly into her ear. "If you didn't own a cupcake shop, this story might have turned out differently."

Feeling as though her spontaneous embrace had crossed a line, she released him quickly and pointed at the hole. "Cupcake is down there."

He stepped forward to inspect the pit.

"Wait." She took the flashlight out of his hand and shined it towards where the rustling sound had been. She saw nothing. She moved the light from side to side but still saw nothing. "I could have sworn something was right there."

He followed her gaze for a moment before dismissing her. "Probably just a deer." He took the flashlight from her and pointed it into the hole. Cupcake thumped her tail and whimpered again. "Well, hi there, little girl." He glanced sideways at Kylie. "Please tell me it's a girl with that name."

Kylie ignored his comment. "Do you think you can get her out?"

"It will be tight, but I think the ladder will fit."

Kylie watched as the chief lowered the ladder, descended, and scooped out the wiggly puppy. As soon as he let go of her, Cupcake jumped on her owner, smothering her with kisses. Kylie laughed and hugged the four-month-old puppy. "Cupcakie, I was so scared! Oh, yes, I was, yes, I was," she repeated to the overjoyed puppy.

She scooped the puppy up and turned to her rescuer. "Listen, I don't usually like to ask people for help, but thank you so much for getting us out of this." She gave the puppy an extra squeeze. "As I said, I didn't know who else to call."

He gave her a modest nod of his head. "I see cupcakes in my future."

She smiled and kissed the puppy again before looking up to him. "I do too. Stop by this week, and I'll set you up."

"And you named your pit bull Cupcake?"

"She's a pit mix," she corrected defensively. She gave the puppy in her arms another kiss. "And what else would I name her?"

He just shook his head and pulled the ladder out of the hole.

"So what do you think this is? An old well?" Now that her fear had subsided, she was curious.

He adjusted his hat with the head lamp on it. "It's pretty shallow for that. I'd guess it's an old air shaft for the club."

Kylie knew he was referring to the home she had purchased. "This far away?"

He shrugged and grinned at her. "If you believe the local stories, yes."

CHAPTER 2

Not wanting to hear any scary stories in the dark woods, Kylie waited until they were back at her house before she turned to the fire chief. "So what are the local stories about this place?" She felt tense as she asked, worried his response may keep her up at night.

The chief looked up at the two-story log cabin building that had been one of the hottest spots for elite resorters in northern Michigan in the late 1920s and '30s. His eyes grew dark as he took in the state of disrepair the building was in and its surroundings. "This is a huge project," he commented, ignoring her question. His eyes continued to scan the massive structure with fieldstone chimneys, dark logs separated by white crumbling joint compound, and tattered awnings. "I can't believe it's even livable inside."

Kylie felt embarrassed. "I just stay in one bedroom and use one bathroom." Her cheeks flushed. "I'm working on it."

"Alone?"

"That's all I can afford." She set the puppy down to scamper about the dark circle drive they stood on by the front door.

"No kitchen?"

"There are two kitchens, but they need some, uh," she hesitated again, embarrassed by her shabby home for the first time, "cleaning." He didn't look like he believed her. "And appliances," she added with a shrug.

"So where do you eat?"

"The shop." She slipped her hands easily into the pockets of her black running pants. "I'm there most of the time anyway."

He nodded in understanding as his eyes continued to view the building warily.

Eager to distract him, she asked again, "So what are the local stories?"

"It's late, and I don't want to alarm you. Why don't I stop by and get a cupcake tomorrow and tell you in the daylight?"

Kylie looked at the building that now looked ominous to her instead of like a family home. "I'm not going back in there until you tell me." She felt a shudder ripple through her. "There's not some demon in there or something, is there?"

The chief smiled, and Kylie could see the light spattering of freckles across his nose and cheeks in the warm glow of the porchlight. "Nah, nothing like that."

She felt relieved again and placed her hands on her hips in determination. "So tell me what the deal is."

He shrugged. "It's just some old legend probably blown way out of proportion. It doesn't mean anything."

"Waiting," she informed him without changing her expectant pose.

He leaned on his ladder. "Folks say there are tunnels that come out of the building."

Kylie's mind took in what he said and processed it for a moment. She looked up at the old building next to her and pushed a strand of her short, white-blonde hair behind an ear. Her eyes moved from one end of the building to the other and then into the dark woods surrounding it. She let out a guffaw. "Well, I've lived here a week and have never seen a tunnel. They'd have to be secret tunnels."

She turned back to the chief and saw him looking at her expectantly as the wave of realization rushed over her. "They're secret tunnels?"

He grinned at her. "Not too much of a secret if folks talk about them."

She looked at him with large eyes. "The realtor never said anything to me."

He shrugged in response.

She thought for a moment. "There's a door behind the bar in the basement that leads to a couple of rooms that the realtor said were once secret rooms used to stash liquor, but there are no tunnels."

The chief shrugged again, holding up his hands. "I'm just passing along information."

She remembered her dog. "Cupcake!" She looked into the darkness for the black dog. "Cupcakie!" she called again. She heard a light clicking of toenails and turned behind her to see the puppy running towards her on the circle drive in a clumsy run owned only by a four-month-old puppy. "Good girl," she said, bending down and scooping the puppy up, giving her a squeeze.

She looked back at the tall chief with sandy brown hair before her. "So do I worry about someone entering through tunnels in the night and killing me?"

He let out a snort of humor. "If you didn't see any tunnels, then they must not be there."

Kylie started to feel relieved when another thought occurred to her. "But what about the hole Cupcake fell in?"

"My guess is it's an old air shaft and nothing more."

She nodded, still looking concerned.

"There was a grate covering the shaft opening in the side of the hole. Not much could fit through it."

Kylie thought again and looked at him with worry. "What about snakes?"

The chief looked at the pretty 31-year-old blonde and decided not to worry her. "I don't think they could fit through the screening of the grate."

"There's a screen?"

"Yeah," he lied in an effort to relieve some of her anxiety, "there was a screen."

She suddenly had an uneasy feeling at the thought of going back into the dark, old building alone. "So the tunnels are the only thing people talk about?"

He shrugged again. He definitely wasn't digging himself any deeper with this. "Pretty much."

She nodded in understanding and took a step back, the puppy still in her arms. "Well, thanks for rescuing me." She saw him smile at her, and she blushed. "I mean Cupcake. Thanks for rescuing Cupcake." She held one of the puppy's paws up to wave at him. "I don't need rescuing."

He reached out and shook the puppy's paw before giving it a scratch on the head that caused her large ears to flop. "Any time, Cupcake."

"And, listen, stop by the shop any time for some cupcakes on the house."

"Thanks." He turned and took a few steps towards his pickup truck before turning back to her. "How did you have my home number anyway?"

Kylie smiled and held up her cell phone. "When people register for my e-mail blast, they give me their phone number."

"And I'm part of your e-mail blast," he acknowledged.

"Yup. You and everyone else in town."

He smiled back. "Well, just everyone else that likes cupcakes."

"There's no such thing as someone who doesn't like cupcakes, Chief," she informed him in a matter-of-fact tone.

"You can call me Jason."

"Don't forget to pick those cupcakes up, Jason," she acknowledged his name. "Cupcake says thanks again for the rescue."

He slid the ladder onto the bed of his truck and closed the tailgate. "It's what I do," he said as he walked to the door of his truck and got in.

He waved out his window before he pulled away, and Kylie lifted Cupcake's white-tipped paw to wave back at her rescuer before turning to face the dark building alone. Her vision of a Christmas tree and a family vanished, and she felt a shiver run up her spine at the thought of entering the old building.

She kissed Cupcake's head. "You'll keep me safe, won't you Cuppie?"

CHAPTER 3

It was a warm spring day in 1930 when Paul Preston and his fellow gang members, Joey and Russ, walked into the lobby of the LaSalle Hotel in Detroit. Paul felt the cold steel in the pocket of his suit, and his head had beads of sweat on it. A conversation from the night before with one of the Purple Gang leaders, Izzy Bernstein, kept running through his mind. "Do this right, and I'll get you out of town safely."

Paul knew that the reign of his gang had climaxed and was now teetering on the brink of downfall. Although the Purple Gang had been engaged in a very lucrative yet unholy alliance with Al Capone, supplying Canadian Whiskey to his organization in Chicago, the St. Valentine's Day Massacre had been a game changer for all of the members. Paul no longer knew who he could trust.

His life of crime had all started when his parents emigrated from Eastern Europe to Detroit twenty-five years ago. Paul and his older brother had been young children at the time, and they'd settled in the poverty-stricken section of Detroit's lower east side.

When they were old enough, he and his brother had been sent to Bishop School, where they'd met and befriended the Bernstein brothers.

In an effort to gain the spending money that their parents never had to give them, the boys had started simply as nothing more than petty thieves; but things quickly progressed once they finished school. Armed robbery, extortion, and hijacking had become the new norm in Paul's life after he finished school. His group was a tight-knit one, and its fingers soon reached outside the boundaries of Detroit, and the gang and its power grew.

With power comes people who will challenge it, and Paul had seen it begin with the Cleaners and Dyers War in 1927. He knew resorting to bombs and arson to control the union members was the gang's only effective choice. Paul lived his life by rules. If the people didn't follow the rules, there were consequences to pay. Crossing paths with Paul was one of those consequences.

Quickly following the Cleaners and Dyers War came the Miraflores Massacre. The Purple Gang had been double-crossed by three of its independent contractors imported from Chicago and New York as enforcers, and Paul was one of those asked to clean things up. It had been his first time using the machine gun that he now kept under the backseat of his car.

The St. Valentine's Day Massacre had been the final straw. Instead of delivering liquor to Chicago, Paul had dressed like a police officer, along with four other men, and used his machine gun again, this time killing seven men. Things were escalating out of control, and Paul was wanted in several states.

It was long after dinner hours when Paul met with his brother Bugs at their family restaurant to ask him a favor. "Just talk to the Bernsteins for me. Tell them I want out of Detroit. I've done everything the brothers have ever asked of me, but my mug is on posters all over town."

Bugs took a slow draw on his cigar and leaned back in the booth at his father's restaurant. "How will they know ya won't rat us out?"

Paul leaned forward on his elbows. "Bugsey, I'm not turning on you. I just need to be somewhere safe." His eyes glanced to the side in search of words before continuing. "Someplace where no one knows me."

Bugs looked at his younger brother and cohort carefully from behind his cloud of smoke. "How do ya think the brothers are going to take that?"

Paul pressed his fingertips together on the tabletop. "Just get me out of town. I've been doing the front-line work for too long. I just need to get out of town."

Bugs watched his younger brother carefully before slowly nodding. "So you want an operation out of town?"

Paul relaxed a little, seeing that Bugs understood. "Yeah. Something small and quiet." He looked down at his hands that had taken so many lives. "Something I can work at for a few years until folks forget me around here."

Bugs squinted at his younger brother and nodded. "I think I

know just the place." He crossed his arms and leaned back. "I'll talk to the brothers and see what they think."

And now here Paul was, performing his final hit for The Purple Gang of Detroit.

"Are you sure you know what he looks like?" Russ asked the other two gang members as the well-dressed men strode casually through the busy upscale lobby.

Paul nodded solemnly. "I'd know him anywhere." His crisp gray suit was framed nicely by his black shoes and fedora.

"Ya sure this will end any chances for the recall of Mayor Bowles?" Joey asked, sounding uncertain.

"Doesn't matter," Paul answered, his cold eyes scanning the lobby for their target. "Orders are orders. What the brothers say to do, we do." He gripped the cold steel in his left pocket tightly, feeling the sweat from his palm make the metal slippery.

"That's him," Joey indicated.

Paul and Russ followed Joey's gaze. The handsome radio

commentator was walking confidently across the lobby, a briefcase in one hand.

"Here we go, fellas," Paul stated as he stepped across the room to meet his victim. Approaching and then holding out a hand, he said, "Mr. Buckley, I'm a big fan."

Jerry Buckley slowed his stride and smiled at the men. "Well, fellas, it's always nice to meet fans." He held out a hand, and Paul recognized his voice from the radio programs he often listened to.

As their right hands met in a handshake, Paul's left hand gripped the cold steel in his pocket and squeezed the trigger, causing a bullet to tear out of the pocket of his tailored suit and into his greeter. The expression on the man's face changed to one of shock and then of pain. A second later, Paul's cohorts shot rounds from their own pockets into the stunned radio personality who had tried to extort money from the gang.

Screams and terror filled the lobby of the LaSalle Hotel as

Jerry Buckley fell to the floor. His assailants didn't stop until eleven shots had been fired, ensuring his death.

With not an ounce of fear showing on his face, Paul and his fellow gang members turned and casually walked out of the lobby with no one in pursuit. They didn't run, and they didn't rush. Witnesses watched in silent shock. Screams filled the room behind them as patrons rushed to the fallen man in an attempt to aid him.

Paul casually slid into the backseat of the Cadillac parked outside the hotel as Joey and Russ filled the front seat. He looked down at the bullet holes in the front pocket of his suit jacket. "I guess this suit is done for."

Joey smirked as he pulled away from the curb. "I hear the suits are provided where you're going."

There were witnesses all over downtown Detroit that could recognize Paul's face and identify him as one of the killers. That very night, he disappeared from Detroit via private plane to an establishment the gang owned in a remote location.

It was one a.m. when Paul stepped off the plane at the Harbor Springs Airport and took a slow draw on his cigarette before dropping the butt on the ground and grinding it out with his foot. He exhaled as he saw a man approaching through the darkness that couldn't be more than eighteen years old.

"You're Mr. Preston, sir?"

Paul let out a slow exhale and nodded.

The young man looked ecstatic and held out his hand. "Wow. Pleased to meet you, sir. You're legend around here."

Paul looked at the hand and hesitated to take it, remembering what had happened to the last man that had extended a hand to him.

The man continued to hold his hand out, his innocence showing on his face. "I'm Willy. I'll be taking you to the club."

Paul looked at the hand again and slowly extended his to meet Willy's. He gave it a slow, firm shake but didn't speak.

Unaffected, Willy continued. "If you have luggage, I can

help you take it to the club."

Paul's eyes scanned his surroundings through the darkness. "Where's the car?"

Willy smiled, relieved that the man was now speaking to him. "No car. We can walk."

Paul turned to look around him again. "We're walking? There are no lights around here." He completed his circle to face Willy. "How far are we walking?"

Willy continued his innocent and excited smile. "Not far, sir. Just a few blocks."

Paul looked around uneasily again. He had a bad feeling about this. His left hand slipped into his front pocket where it landed on the cold steel he kept there. It was loaded, but would there be enough rounds to take care of a crowd? He gripped the handle. Something told him things weren't right.

Willy stepped forward and took the suitcase that the attendant handed him from the small plane. "Is this it?"

Paul looked at the one suitcase that sadly summed up his life and nodded.

Still excited, Willy tilted his head towards the darkness beyond. "Let's go."

His hand remaining in his pocket, Paul followed the young man across the air strip, his senses at full alert. The only sounds around him were from crickets. A couple of hangars reflected the moonlight and lit Paul's way. His eyes desperately searched the darkness.

He followed Willy behind the hangars and to a hillside. Willy led the way through the thick underbrush, holding back saplings and large bushes for Paul.

Frustrated, Paul stopped his march. "Boy, where are you taking me?" He was used to downtown Detroit, not crawling through some forest in the dark while dressed in a suit.

Willy held back another sapling and waited. "It's just ahead, sir."

Not sure where else to go, Paul followed the lad for another hundred yards through bushes and trees. Finally, he saw the young man pull something from his pocket before disappearing into utter darkness.

Still clenching the steel in his pocket, Paul paused his walk. "Boy, where are you?"

There was no verbal response. Instead, he saw a match light before a lantern ignited and lit the opening where the boy stood. Willy smiled proudly at the Detroiter. "It's through here."

"We're going to a club through a cave?"

Willy held open the heavy door of black grating. "It's not a cave, it's a tunnel." He turned and started to lead the way into the dark tunnel. When he didn't hear Paul's footsteps behind him, he turned and looked back. Still smiling with innocent confidence, he continued, "Some call this the employee entrance."

CHAPTER 4

Kylie now looked at her house in a different light. She set Cupcake down, and the two walked inside as the headlights of Chief Lange's pickup truck faded quickly into the forest behind them. Her mind was flying. Sure, she had considered it unusual that the basement was nearly twice the size of the house above it. The realtor had told her that a portion of the club had been destroyed by a fire in the late '60s, and she had assumed that was the reason for the larger foundation.

Her mind continued to fly as she walked into what had once been a commercial kitchen that now consisted of a sink and a long island countertop that ran down the center of the room to the door. Knowing the only reason they came into the room was for her food, Cupcake quickly sat next to the portion of the counter that housed her treat jar.

Kylie lifted the lid to the glass cookie jar and pulled out one of the homemade dog treats, momentarily holding it to her chin in thought. She was sure the weird tunnel going from the basement and coming up into her side yard had once been an exterior entrance to the club, so that wouldn't explain the larger foundation.

Cupcake let out a yip for her treat, and Kylie's attention came back to the present.

"Good sit, Cupcake." She leaned over and gave the pup her treat while stroking her black head. "What a good girl."

Cupcake inhaled the peanut butter treat that Kylie had made and sat expectantly looking up at the human.

Kylie smiled. "One is enough, Cupcake. Ready for bedtime?"

Cupcake stayed where she was, knowing this would raise her chances of getting a second treat.

Kylie hesitated before leaving the room. "Well, you did have a near-death experience tonight, Cupcake." She reached back into the jar and pulled out another bone-shaped treat and gave it to the still-sitting dog. "I guess you deserve a little emotional eating."

She walked to the doorway from the kitchen to the dining

room, leaning on it and looking into the room with new interest. It seemed odd to her that this had once been the hottest club in northern Michigan. The realtor had told her that big names like The Beach Boys and Chubby Checker had performed here in the '60s.

Her eyes scoured the room for something that might lead to a secret tunnel, but the walls were white and plain. There were no bookshelves or paintings that could hide something. She could feel the energy of a once-bustling club still lingering.

Cupcake stood next to her owner, looking into the room. Kylie looked down at her. "As long as it's not haunted, I'm okay with tunnels."

Cupcake scampered to the stairs.

"You don't think there are ghosts, do you, Cuppie?"

Cupcake didn't respond and just waited expectantly for her owner.

Kylie left the dining room and scooped the puppy up before ascending the staircase. "I think we have some exploring to do tomorrow," she whispered to the puppy before giving it a light kiss on the head.

Kylie had been baking for four hours the next morning before her Aunt Judy arrived to open the shop.

"Good morning, favorite niece," the woman cheerfully greeted her only niece.

"Good morning, favorite aunt," Kylie greeted her back without looking up from swirling frosting onto a cupcake with a pastry bag.

Judy wove behind the front counter, baking tables, and equipment in the two-room gingerbread house located just off of Main Street in downtown Harbor Springs. "What's the cupcake du jour?" she asked as she arrived in the back office to see Cupcake laying in her usual spot on the desk so she could look through the large glass window into the bakery where her owner worked.

"Cherry cupcake with a cherry and balsamic filling, topped with a vanilla bean frosting."

Judy slipped her purse under the desk, gave Cupcake a pat on the head, and stepped back into the bakery. "Lord, I don't know how you keep coming up with these weird combinations. Balsamic as in vinegar?"

Kylie smiled as she nodded at the older woman with the chin-length banged bob cut. "It's what I do," she responded before realizing it was what Chief Lange had said to her the night before.

Judy moved back to the front of the room, pulled out the chalkboard for the sidewalk, and began writing the daily cupcake special on it. "You know, you're going to need a bigger desk when Cupcake grows into a full grown cake."

Kylie smiled adoringly at the dog whose head rested on her large front paws as she stared back at her owner. "We'll cross that bridge when we get to it." She lifted the large tray of cupcakes and slipped it into the front display case. "Speaking of Cupcake, she had quite a scare last night."

Judy looked at her niece, concern written all over her face.

"What happened?"

Kylie leaned on the display case as she spoke to her aunt writing on the other side of it. "She fell into some kind of air shaft when we were out running last night. Had to call Chief Lange to fish her out."

Judy stood to look at her niece. "Air shaft? In the woods?"

Kylie looked calmly at her aunt, trying to gauge how much she actually knew. "Seems there's some local lore about secret tunnels going out of my place. Know anything about that?"

Judy had lived in the small town her entire life, and Kylie had moved in with her a few years earlier, staying with her until she had enough money saved up to buy her own place. Judy shrugged. "Well, yeah, but I gave it as much weight as I do Bigfoot stories."

Kylie looked alarmed. "There are Bigfoot stories?"

Judy rolled her eyes. "Just the sighting out by Sturgeon Bay, but you're missing my point."

Kylie thought about the loud noises in the woods the night

before and felt nervous perspiration break out on her chest before she changed her focus. "So you've heard the stories?"

"Sure, but they're just stories. Used to be stories about a tunnel from The Harbor Inn to the casino behind it too. Doesn't mean it's there."

Judy stepped out the front door and set the sandwich board chalkboard near the sidewalk before Kylie could continue her questioning.

"So why all of the tunnel stories?"

The older woman thought a moment. "These places were built during Prohibition. I guess people thought they needed ways to smuggle things in and ways to escape."

"Have you ever seen the tunnels?"

Judy walked to the side of the counter and took an apron off the hook before slipping it over her head, careful to avoid her large eyeglasses. "Nope. But I've never seen Bigfoot either."

Kylie rolled her eyes.

"Have you ever seen any tunnels?" the woman fired the same question to her niece.

"No."

She slapped her hands on her heavy thighs. "Well, there you have it. If anyone would see them, it would be someone who lives there."

"So did you ever go to Club Manitou when it was open?"

Judy placed her hands on her hips. "Kylie Sue, I'm not that old."

Kylie blushed.

Judy smiled a half smile and wrapped the apron straps around her robust body, tying them in front. "But your great grandfather used to work there for a while."

Kylie's eyes opened wide. "What? Grandpa Bill?"

Judy nodded. "That's the story."

"And you didn't feel the need to tell me that before I bought the place?"

She shrugged. "It was just a job for a couple of years until Prohibition ended. Then everything changed out there."

"That's when it became abandoned, right?"

The older woman leaned one arm on the counter and placed the other hand on her hip as she thought. "It was abandoned for years until it became The Ponytail Club."

"Oh, right," Kylie remembered. "That's the new addition that burned down, right?"

Her aunt pointed a finger at her and winked. "You got it. Now can we sell some cupcakes?"

Kylie's head was spinning as she filled and frosted the last batch of cupcakes for the day. Apparently she'd moved into some kind of local landmark that was filled with secrets.

CHAPTER 5

Kylie arrived home from the shop after lunch and just in time for the delivery of her new gas range and refrigerator.

"I'm so excited to finally be able to eat at home," she gushed to the delivery men as they rolled the refrigerator in on a dolly.

The two men didn't comment as they maneuvered the heavy appliance into the kitchen before lowering the large, cardboard box. A plumber had already unpacked the gas range and was tinkering with its connections.

"Looks like there's another shut-off valve in the basement I'll need to get to before this thing can turn on." He stood from behind the large appliance to inform Kylie.

"Yeah, I can take you down there," Kylie offered.

She silently led the tall, red-headed plumber down the stairs and into the first room. She flicked a switch on the wall to illuminate it before moving into the second room where she flicked another switch. "I think the line comes down over there, just before the old incinerator." She pointed to a thin pipe running down the wall next to a built-in incinerator with a fourteen-by-fourteen-inch opening.

The plumber didn't move, his eyes instead taking in the ramshackle surroundings. The room was dark and damp. A multitude of pipes ran across the ceiling and walls, and a couple had fallen and lay useless on the back wall.

"This was the downstairs kitchen at one time," Kylie informed him in a tone that told him that's the reason it was in such disarray.

"What's with the safe?" the plumber asked, pointing to a corner of the room.

Kylie shrugged. "It came with the place. I guess it's left from when it used to be a club."

He nodded before smiling and almost sarcastically asking, "Anything in it?"

Not having looked inside the slightly-ajar door before, Kylie strode easily across the room, Cupcake on her heels, and pulled open the door of the four-foot tall safe with a large combination lock on the front. "Doesn't look like it." She pulled out her cell phone and switched on its flashlight. "Nope, no hidden treasure."

She looked up at the plumber, who had already moved on to other things. "And what's up with that?" He pointed to the doorway across the room.

"What's up with what?" she asked, not seeing anything more than what appeared to be a reinforced concrete wall.

He stepped across the room and examined the top of the doorway in the dim light before reaching to the left, hooking his fingers around a portion of the wall that jutted out eight inches, and slid the large, concrete door over the opening.

Kylie gasped.

The plumber stood back proudly and examined his discovery. "Pretty amazing."

Kylie's mind was flying again. "So do you think the area

behind that was one of the secret tunnels people talk about?"

The plumber slid the concrete door back and stepped into the room behind it. "Nope. Those stairs over there go outside to a main entrance. Not much of a secret."

Kylie nodded, still looking around.

The plumber crossed the room to the base of the stairs. "I'm sure you've noticed this." He pointed to the large, steel door on sliders, set so it would cover the stairwell in an emergency, keeping intruders at bay.

"Yes," Kylie confirmed. "That one is a little more obvious."

He slid the door closed and then slid it open again. Cupcake yipped at the door as if moving it was some sort of game to her.

The plumber chuckled. "Pretty cool."

"Yeah," Kylie agreed, her eyes searching the walls for other secrets that she might have missed.

The room was quiet as the plumber's eyes also moved

carefully over the walls. Seeing nothing, he stepped through the door to his left and peered into what had been the area where the bands had performed. A small stage was built into the wall on his right. His eyes took in the damp floor before moving to the large, double-sided fieldstone fireplace that sat in the middle of the room dividing it. "Wow, this place is something else."

Kylie followed him, wondering if he'd discover anything else she'd missed in the dismal basement. "So do you think any of the secret tunnels people talk about are down here?"

He strode casually through the large room, under one of the stone archways that framed either side of the fireplace, and into the area where the remnants of a bar remained. He crossed to his right and opened one of the doors to a rest room, looked around, and stepped back out. "These are eight-inch thick cement block walls. This isn't the type of place you make a secret tunnel."

"Well, you found the cement door in the other room," Kylie pointed out, now feeling doubtful of his quick dismissal of the theory.

"But it stood out from the wall, so I could see it." He looked into the open doors of once-hidden rooms behind the bar area as he put his hands into his pants pockets and strolled through a doorway that led him back to the room with the safe, completing a full-circle tour of the layout. "Nope. This place is built like a fortress, but I think the only secret you have down here is maybe some black mold," he changed his focus from the shut-off valve he had approached to Kylie, "which I would have someone look at, if I were you."

"Great," Kylie mumbled, unhappy at the thought of another expense.

CHAPTER 6

Paul Preston hesitated as he studied Willy holding a lantern in one hand and holding the door of heavy grating open with the other. No one had said anything to him about this. If they were trying to get rid of him, this would be the perfect place to do it.

"Come on, Mr. Preston," Willy urged. "Things will be winding down at the club soon, and Mr. Gerhart told me to bring you straight up to his office."

Paul recognized Al's name. He'd met Al a few times when he'd worked as a driver for the gang before being moved north to run the speakeasy that further expanded the fingers of control for The Purple Gang.

Still grasping the piece of metal in the bullet-torn left pocket of his suit jacket, he lifted his suitcase from where Willy had left it and stepped past the large grate door and into the tunnel.

Willy pulled the heavy grate closed and latched it before holding up his lantern to illuminate the tunnel before them.

Paul drew in a breath as he took in his surroundings. Before him lay an arched tunnel lined entirely in cobblestone. Roots hung through the ceiling, making the passage look old and unstable.

"This way," Willy instructed with confidence.

Paul followed silently, his hard-soled shoes making a sharp sound on the cobblestones that echoed. They'd only traveled a hundred yards when Paul heard a loud noise above them that caused the tunnel to shake and bits of dirt to drop from the ceiling. Instinctively, Paul ducked and held an arm up to protect himself. "Jesus! Where are you taking me?"

Willy chuckled with confidence. "That always happens when the trucks drive over."

"Trucks?" Paul straightened. "We're under a road?"

Willy started walking again, and Paul followed. "Yep. It's M-131, the Harbor-Petoskey Road," he clarified," so there's a decent amount of traffic. The heavy trucks are what really shake things up down here though."

"I noticed," Paul muttered to himself unhappily.

Another fifty yards, and Paul heard music ahead. "Sounds like we're getting close," he commented more to himself than Willy.

Willy stopped walking, and Paul noticed a cement block wall barricading the tunnel as Willy hung the lantern on a heavy steel hook. "We're here, Mr. Preston."

Paul looked confused but stood by silently and watched as Willy easily slipped his fingers into an indented handle of the cement wall and casually pulled it open as if he did this sort of thing every day. Light, loud music, and the sounds of laughter streamed through the opening.

Willy blew out the lantern, leaned to take Paul's suitcase from his hand, and stepped forward. "You have to duck to fit under these shelves," he apologized as he led the way.

Paul followed Willy, stepping into a small room with shelves of liquor bottles lining the wall opposite him. The wall he had stepped through had shelves filled with poker chips and cards. A

Roulette table stood at the end, making the space feel tight. "It's one of our safe rooms in case of a raid," Willy informed as he quickly pulled the cement block wall closed behind him, filling the gap in the shelves. He set the suitcase down momentarily as he moved two shelves of poker chips back into place, making the tunnel entrance completely unnoticeable.

Lifting the suitcase again, he turned and leaned against another cement block wall and listened. He grinned impishly at his guest. "This is the fun part." He listened again, determined it was clear, and pushed the cement block wall in front of him open. He turned and beckoned quickly to Paul. "Ever been in a ladies room?"

Paul had stopped trying to comprehend what was going on in this surreal setting when they'd first entered the tunnel, so he just followed silently into the pink wallpapered ladies room.

Willy easily pushed the door closed, what seemed to be the seams of the wallpaper hiding any trace of the door they had stepped through. Turning to his guest, Willy patted him on the arm. "Let's get going before someone comes in to use it," he winked with a grin.

Paul smirked and followed the boy out of the room and into a club filled with loud music, laughter, and smoke.

CHAPTER 7

"You're late," Kylie called when she heard the jingle of the shop's bell.

"Late for what?"

Not hearing the voice she'd expected, Kylie spun around to see Chief Lange standing at the front counter of her cupcake shop. His large frame blocked the doorway right behind him, and Kylie noticed his broad shoulders and strong arms in the navy blue T-shirt and pants he wore as a uniform.

She blushed. "Sorry. I thought you were my Aunt Judy."

He crossed his strong arms. "Yeah, we look a lot alike."

"Well, I didn't recognize you without your firefighter hat on," she weakly defended with a smile.

He let out a snort. "Because otherwise we'd look exactly the same?"

Her eyes moved up to his short sandy brown hair brushed

neatly to the side. "Well, maybe if you had bangs," she teased.

He shook his head forlornly. "I'd better stop while I'm ahead."

Kylie giggled. "Looking for those cupcakes I promised you?"

He dropped his arms and leaned them on the display case, keeping his gaze on her. "That, and I thought I'd follow up and see how the victim was recovering."

Kylie pointed to the office window at the back of the shop where Cupcake stood watching her rescuer with a wagging tail. "I'd say she's recovered a hundred percent."

"Good to hear," the Chief approved as his focus left the puppy and moved back to the shop owner. "And how are you holding up out there all alone?"

Kylie shrugged. "Better now that I've had some kitchen appliances delivered."

"Good. Glad to hear it," he smiled at her, his eyes meeting hers.

Feeling an awkward silence, Kylie cleared her throat and pulled out a box to put cupcakes in. "So what would you like?"

His eyes moved to the case as he perused his choices. "Love Spell?" he questioned. "What's in Love Spell?"

It's a nutmeg cupcake with a cinnamon-butter filling topped with juniper berry frosting."

"Juniper berries? Aren't those poisonous?"

"I'm sure you've had a form of them in drinks before, and you're still here, so I guess not."

"Huh?"

"Gin's predominant flavor comes from juniper berries."

He looked impressed. "You're pretty knowledgeable, Miss Cupcake."

Kylie smiled. "However, I wouldn't recommend giving cupcakes filled with an ancient love spell to the men at the firehouse." She saw him blush before continuing. "People might start to talk."

"So how did you get into the cupcake business?"

Kylie folded the edges of the box as she spoke. "I studied to become a pastry chef out east." She tucked the ends of the box together. "I had always loved visiting Aunt Judy here in the summers; so, when she retired and suggested we open a shop together, I jumped at the opportunity."

The chief continued to gaze into the case, avoiding eye contact for his next question. "Ever married?"

"Nope. I was always moving around, working in different restaurants. I never really put down roots." She kept her focus on the box, equally avoiding eye contact.

"Until now," he looked up at her as he stated his conclusion.

She set the finished box on top of the display case that separated them. "And how about you?" she asked without directly replying to his comment.

He took his elbows off of the display case, standing to his full height. "Born and raised in Harbor. I'll probably die here, too, if I have anything to say about it."

"Well, I guess that would explain why you know all of the local stories."

"Any questions, I'm the guy to ask," he said proudly pointing a thumb to his chest.

Their eyes held again, and there was another awkward moment of silence. Kylie cleared her throat. "So what did you decide on?"

"Huh?"

"For cupcakes," she indicated to the display case.

He looked back at the display case and read the labels again. "Don't you have plain chocolate or vanilla?"

"No," she responded, the tone of her voice indicating she'd been slightly offended. "You can find those at your local grocery store. I like people to expect the unexpected."

"Touchy," he mumbled, looking down and still trying to decide on a flavor. "Balsamic cherry? Lemon basil coconut? Tomato herb with a tomato butter?" He shook his head. "Maybe you'd better suggest something that all the guys will like."

Kylie looked down at the display case. "Everyone likes chocolate. I'd recommend the salted caramel cupcake."

"Where's the chocolate?"

"I put a homemade salted chocolate caramel inside of the caramel cupcake and then top it with caramel frosting and sprinkled flakes of salt."

He shook his head. "Mel's not that into sweets. Plus, the caramel might pull out one of his fakes." He gestured to his teeth.

Kylie started boxing up the salted caramel cupcakes. "So we'll add one tomato herb cupcake for Mel." She tied a string around the box and pushed it forward as the Chief reached into his pocket and fumbled with his wallet. "As I said, it's on the house." She looked at him shyly as she continued. "Thanks for rescuing

Cupcake."

"Thanks. I'm sure the guys will – " He was interrupted by the crackle of his radio.

"We have a female down at 223 Main Street. Immediate assistance required."

Chief Lange's muscles tightened as he lifted the radio from his waistband to his mouth and turned to the door. "Got it. On my way. Tell Mel I'll meet him there."

In a flash, he was out the door, leaving the box of cupcakes on the counter and a stunned Kylie.

"223 Main Street?" she mumbled to herself. "Aunt Judy!"

She darted around the counter to lock the front door and turn the sign on it to read "Closed." Untying her apron as she ran to the office, she snatched up the puppy standing on her desk and ran out the back door.

Judy was lying on a stretcher that was being wheeled out of her white house with green shutters in downtown Harbor Springs.

Chief Lange stood at the head and Mel, a firefighter Kylie had seen around town, was at the opposite end.

"Aunt Judy!" Kylie called as she ran to the stretcher, leaving a yipping puppy in the car. As she approached, she could see the pain that twisted the older woman's face. "Aunt Judy, what happened?" she asked, trotting alongside the stretcher.

"I slipped, Kylie." Her eyes winced in pain. "I think I broke something."

The two men had reached the ambulance and lowered the legs of the stretcher before lifting it into the vehicle.

"What should I do?" Kylie asked her aunt in panic.

Turning to her as Mel got in and closed the doors, Chief Lange put an arm on her shoulder. "Don't panic. We're taking her to Northern Michigan Hospital. You can meet us in the Emergency Room."

Kylie nodded, the surprise and shock of the situation numbing her and making her slow to both think and move.

CHAPTER 8

Phyllis held the ends of her fox fur in an effort to balance herself as she stepped out of the brand-new 1930 Cadillac Sixteen's door held open by the valet. She and her husband Henry had arrived in Harbor Springs via train the week before for the summer season. The days were delightfully comfortable compared to the heat in the City of Detroit, and the evenings were chilly due in large part to the damp lake air.

The valet extended his hand to her, and she gave him a small smile of appreciation as she silently accepted it before reaching for her husband's waiting arm to walk into Club Manitou.

"So this is it?" she asked, looking up at the two-story log structure that sported red and gold striped awnings over every window and the main entrance.

"This is it," her husband assured as he patted her hand holding his arm.

"It looks so," she hesitated, searching for the right word,

"rustic."

Henry looked at his much-younger wife. "We're in the north now, sweetheart. Rustic is all they do here."

Phyllis smiled weakly at her husband before allowing him to lead her up the three steps to the main entrance, covered by a long awning that extended down the entire side of the building.

"Good evening," they were greeted by a tall maître d' in a white sport jacket and black bow tie just inside the door.

"Good evening," her husband replied.

"Name on the reservation?"

"Henry Fairfield and wife."

The maître d' glanced at Phyllis out of the corner of his eye, and she tightened her grip on her husband's arm. "Here we are," he pointed to the reservation on the book. Still writing and looking down, he casually asked, "And how did you hear about us?"

"Joe Walsh said we would enjoy it."

The maître d's face lit up in recognition. "Ah, yes, I know Mr. Walsh well. In that case, you may also enjoy our band downstairs after your dinner if you so choose."

Henry tipped his fedora in gratitude.

As the maître d' led them to a table, he pointed to a young man standing near an exit. "That's Willy. He will escort you downstairs whenever you choose."

Hours later, Phyllis walked over to the bar in the basement speakeasy and placed her tea cup on it. "I'll have a refill, please."

"Are you enjoying your visit?" the maître d' asked as he slid his elbows onto the bar next to her.

She shrugged, unimpressed, before gesturing to the Roulette table. "My husband is."

He glanced at the tea cup as it was slid back to her. "Are you drinking gin?"

She shrugged guiltily and lifted the cup to her lips covered in dark red lipstick.

"Not every day you find a woman that drinks gin straight up," he commented.

She looked at him, surprised he had the nerve to point out her escape from reality. She pushed one of her short, brown waves behind an ear and looked back to the cup before responding. "It's not every day you find a woman like me."

Paul's eyes ran down her lithe frame appreciatively and back up to her sad eyes. "No, not every day," he replied. Turning to the bartender, he told him, "This one's on the house, Scotty."

Phyllis looked at him in surprise as he slapped his hand on the bar, threw her an understanding smile, and walked away.

Weeks later, Phyllis and Henry had become regulars at Club Manitou. At every visit, Paul bought the lonely bride a drink as she sat at the bar and her husband gambled the evening away.

Tonight he slid a quarter across the bar to her.

Leaning on her elbows and holding her tea cup with two hands, Phyllis looked down at the coin. "And what am I supposed to do with that?"

The man in the white jacket didn't speak but instead gestured to the slot machine setting at the end of the bar.

She let out a whispered guffaw of dismissal. "Trying to create an addict, are you?"

Leaning on one elbow to face her, he wove his fingers together. "Maybe I'm just trying to make you smile."

She glanced at him and then straight ahead, watching him in the bar's mirror. "Why would you care if I smile? Don't you have other customers to attend to?"

"I do." He separated his hands, fished around in his pants pocket, and produced another quarter that he pushed across the bar to lay next to the last.

She held back a smile, not wanting to give the stranger the satisfaction. "What's your name?"

He likewise held back a smile. "Paul Preston."

"Are you opposed to gin?"

"Not a bit," he responded, pulling a box of cigarettes from his top jacket pocket. He held it out to her first in offering.

Phyllis leaned to look around her new acquaintance and into the game room where her husband was enjoying the evening at the Roulette table with strangers. She looked back at the man next to her and nodded softly before taking one.

Pulling a box of matches from his pocket along with it, he pushed a third quarter across the bar. "Oops, what do we have here?"

Now she couldn't hold back her smile and shook her head. "Just light the damn cigarette."

Paul smirked in satisfaction before lighting one for himself. "So where ya from?"

"Detroit," she momentarily held in the smoke as she spoke before exhaling.

He nodded solemnly. "Me too."

She cocked her head at him as if she wondered why he thought that was relevant.

"I came up here for work," he continued, pretending not to notice her lack of interest.

"Aren't there enough jobs for waiters in Detroit?" she asked in a condescending tone.

He smirked again, confident. It amused him to see how she assumed things about him and then so readily dismissed him. "I run the place with Al Gerhart."

She nodded and took another hit off the cigarette, uninterested.

An awkward silence ensued before Paul pushed the three quarters closer to her.

She smirked and shook her head. "Oh, fine," she gave in, placing her cigarette on an ashtray.

At the end of the bar, she stood facing the machine, Paul leaning on the bar to face her.

"How do I work this thing?" She stood holding a quarter ready but unsure how to proceed.

"See that big slot in the front?" He kept his hands folded as he spoke.

She looked at him with irritation but stuck the quarter in the slot. She lifted her right hand to the large handle on the side of the machine as she'd seen others do. "And now I just pull this?"

"You're a natural," he replied sarcastically.

She threw him a small smile again before pulling the handle. The pieces of fruit on the machine spun around, and Phyllis waited expectantly. Seconds ticked by before she stomped her foot. "Ugh, what a waste of money."

Paul slid another quarter on the machine nearer to her hand.

She hesitated to glance at him before taking it. "You are trying to create an addict," she mumbled.

This time when the pieces of fruit flew by they stopped on

two cherries and a flame. The machine began to ding, and eight quarters fell out into the tray at its base. "I won! I won!" she shouted in excitement as she gathered her payout.

Paul watched her with satisfaction written across his face but said nothing.

She turned to him, her face bright with excitement as she held out the quarters. "Did you see I won?"

Paul kept the satisfied look on his face as his eyes held hers. "Like I said, you're a natural."

CHAPTER 9

Cupcake's toenails clicked on the polished floor of the Harbor Bluffs Care Facility. Knowing the way to Judy's room, Cupcake tugged on the leash, leading the way. "Slow down, Cupcakie," Kylie giggled as she rounded the corner to Judy's room and saw Chief Lange at her bedside. A bouquet consisting of hydrangeas and a couple of roses brightened the room.

"Kylie, come on in," Judy called when she saw her niece out of the corner of her eye.

Letting go of the leash, Kylie let Cupcake run across the room and jump onto the bed, covering Judy's face with puppy kisses.

"Chief – Jason," Kylie greeted, correcting herself.

"Hey, Kylie," he replied, but his focus was on the puppy as he leaned over and scratched her head before she snuggled into the bed, making herself comfortable.

"You came to visit Aunt Judy?"

"I try to stay in touch with the locals." He turned to face her, leaning on the headboard and crossing his arms, humor twinkling in his green eyes. "Are those for me?"

Kylie looked down at the large string-tied box in her hands. "No, they're for – I mean, yes, if you want one, but I brought them for the staff."

He smiled at her flustered expression. "That's okay, I wouldn't want to accidentally get the Love Spell cupcake."

"Oh, I'm sure there are worse things that could happen to you," Judy finally chimed in, still stroking a happy puppy's head.

Now it was Kylie's turn to smirk as she set the large box on the end table and sat in the empty chair. "How are you feeling, Aunt Judy?"

"Oh, they have me in therapy twice a day, and I should be able to go home at the end of the week."

"I've seen broken hips before," Chief Lange commented, "but multiple breaks, well, that's a new one for me."

"Leave it to me to set new records," Judy commented from the bed. "How's the shop running without me, Kylie?"

"Fine, fine," Kylie assured her aunt. "I've got one of the high school kids running the counter until you come back, so don't worry yourself, just get well."

"Well, I'm feeling very motivated to get home," she looked down at the dozing puppy as she spoke. "I never knew people still made Jell-o."

Chief Lange chuckled. "Maybe you can get them to swap out cupcakes for Jell-o," he suggested. "Just keep that Love Spell away from them. Can you imagine if that got into the hands of these people?"

Kylie smiled. "You're really hung up on the Love Spell thing, aren't you?"

"Well, I just wouldn't want to accidentally eat one."

"God forbid," Judy rolled her eyes from the bed.

Kylie changed the topic. "Hey, thanks for getting to my Aunt

Judy so quickly. I – we," she glanced at her aunt, "really appreciate it."

"It's what I do," he repeated his usual line.

"Well, thank you," she offered softly.

He nodded his head as an awkward silence set in. "So I'd better get back to the station. Judy, glad to see you're doing well." He gave her leg a light pat before stepping away.

He gave Cupcake another scratch on the head and stepped towards the door before turning back to Kylie. "Oh, and the fellas at the station really liked the cupcakes. You were right about Mel, he's all about tomato cupcakes now."

Kylie blushed at the compliment.

He tapped his large hand on the door frame. "Weirdest thing I've ever heard of, but thanks."

"You're welcome," Kylie smiled. "It's what I do," she mimicked his previous comment.

He winked at her before leaving the doorway.

"I think he likes you," Judy whispered from her bed once the females were alone in the room.

Kylie let a short breath of air escape her lips in dismissal. "He's just doing his job, Aunt Judy."

"Surely you don't think he visits every person he rescues."

"It's not like there are so many people in this town that that's hard to believe."

The older woman shrugged. "I just thought I'd mention it." She smiled mischievously. "It doesn't hurt that he looks good both coming and going."

"Aunt Judy!" Kylie chastised her aunt as she blushed. "Besides," she continued, "I'm sure every woman in town is throwing herself at him in hopes of having her very own superhero."

"Seems like he's rescued Cupcake and me," she looked back down at the puppy on her bed.

"And I'm not saying that's not handy but, as he said, it's just his job."

"Okay," the woman in bed responded, sounding unconvinced.

"I mean it's not like he'd go around rescuing people if it weren't his job. Besides," Kylie finished her defense, "I don't need rescuing."

"Hmm. You never know," Aunt Judy commented, still looking at the dozing puppy.

Kylie shook her head and changed the subject. "So do you need me to do anything at your house or pick anything up?"

"If you've watered the plants, then you've done it all," she commented in a tone that sounded a little bit empty.

"Okay." Kylie gently placed her palms on her thighs before pushing herself up. "I've got to get back to the shop. Make sure the staff get their cupcakes when they come in."

"Just to be safe, you didn't put any Love Spell cupcakes in

there, did you?" her aunt asked with a concerned expression on her face.

"Aunt Judy," Kylie rolled her eyes.

"I just wouldn't want that Sam Shepard down the hall to get any ideas."

"Isn't he married?"

"Widowed."

"Ah. Well, I'll take that as a request for one Love Spell cupcake next time I come in."

"Oh, God, no," she looked horrified. "I wouldn't want some retired librarian walking around talking about books all the time." She thought again for a moment. "Besides, unlike Chief Lange, Sam only looks good going."

Kylie smiled as her aunt adjusted her large glasses to emphasize her eye roll. She leaned in and gave her a hug, simultaneously lifting the sleeping puppy from the bed. "You're something else, Aunt Judy. See you in a couple of days."

Cupcake's toenails clicked back down the hallway as she pulled Kylie along. Residents in wheelchairs in the hall smiled or held out a hand to the puppy, who more than happily obliged.

They were slowly working their way out when Kylie heard a weak voice say, "Oh, a puppy."

Following the sound, Kylie stopped and looked into a room where a very old woman with below-shoulder-length gray hair sat in a wheelchair with the TV on.

"Puppy," she repeated, holding a hand down.

Never one to deny a pat on the head, Cupcake tugged her leash out of Kylie's hand and ran to the lowered hand.

"Cupcakie!" Kylie weakly chastised. She followed her into the room and sat down next to the woman.

"Cupcake is a cute name," the woman commented without looking up from the dog.

"Thanks," Kylie watched the woman. "I own Kylie Kakes, the cupcake shop in town, so it seemed to go with the theme of my life lately."

"A cupcake shop?" she sounded interested and then looked sad. "I've been in here so long that I don't even know what's going on in town anymore."

"I see you've met our local centenarian," an attendant stopped in the doorway. "Everything okay, Madeline?"

Madeline straightened in her chair to reply. "Yes, I'm fine."

Cupcake left her new friend and scampered across the small room to grace the attendant with her attention. "Well, hi," the woman in scrubs leaned over to pet the puppy.

"Her name is Cupcake," Madeline informed the attendant. "Isn't that cute?"

"Well, hello, Cupcake. Did you make a new friend?"

Cupcake licked the woman's hand.

Kylie looked at Madeline. "Centenarian? You're a hundred years old?"

"And three months," the woman informed.

"And she's going strong, aren't you, Madeline?" the attendant scooped up the puppy and returned her to the patient.

"Well, not as strong as I was twenty years ago," Madeline commented dryly. Looking up at the puppy in the nurse's arms and smiling, she asked Kylie, "May I hold her on my lap?"

Kylie shrugged. "Sure."

The attendant placed the wiggly puppy in the centenarian's lap, and Cupcake took the opportunity to lick the old woman's face.

"You might be sorry you requested that," Kylie apologized. "She's a kisser."

The woman was smiling. "That's okay, I like puppy kisses." She kissed the puppy back, much to Cupcake's delight.

"I'll check back with you in a while, Madeline," the attendant informed.

The woman nodded, focusing on the puppy kisses she was

getting. Kylie watched in silence for a few moments before the woman spoke. "Did you know that you get a birthday card from the President when you turn a hundred years old?"

"No, I didn't." Kylie's eyes moved around the room, looking for a card.

As if sensing what she was searching for, the woman continued. "It's in my scrapbook."

Kylie nodded, her mind searching for something to talk about. "So where did you live in town?"

"Pine Street."

Kylie nodded, wondering what else to ask the woman.

Madeline looked up from the puppy and focused on Kylie. "Where do you live?"

"Well, I was living with my Aunt Judy for a couple of years on Main Street. I just got my own place just outside of town, over near the airport."

"On Mink Road?"

"No, closer to town," Kylie continued. "It used to be the old Gerhart place."

Madeline's eyes darkened. "The Old Club Manitou?"

Kylie perked up. "So you've heard of it?"

Madeline nodded and looked back at the puppy who had settled down in her lap now. "My first love worked there."

CHAPTER 10

Paul watched Phyllis from across the room as she dropped coin after coin into the slot machine. Indeed, he had created an addict. Her pearl-white dress with a collar of small ruffles contrasted beautifully with her lightly-tanned skin.

He looked across the room to her husband, who sat with a drink in his hand at the Roulette table just as he did every night after dinner, mindlessly leaving his young wife to entertain herself.

"Roll a lucky seven for me," Paul heard Henry tell one of the young, blonde cigarette girls at his side over the loud music.

The woman, looking at Henry with stars in her eyes, kissed the dice provocatively before rolling them. "Seven, I rolled a seven!" she squealed in delight before turning to the married man. "I must be good luck for you."

The club music overrode any response Paul could hear as Henry spoke softly to the giggling blonde. He saw Henry look at the woman's hair and push one of the waves in the short-cut bob into place. The woman's hand fluttered to the strand self-consciously, making sure it was in place.

Paul shook his head and looked back at Henry's wife as she stood at the slot machine with her tea cup of gin, seeming to enjoy any distraction from her life.

He strode under the stone archway that separated the basement game room from Slim's Lounge and leaned on the bar next to the woman at the slot machine. "Any luck tonight?"

"No," she pouted, "and I feel just wretched about it."

He gave his head a short tilt to indicate a stool at the bar. "Why don't you take a break and talk to me."

She dropped another quarter into the machine, ignoring his suggestion to sit. "Why would I want to talk to you?"

He smirked again. She was definitely not like other women. "Maybe the machine needs a rest."

That caught her attention. "Do you find you're more likely to win if it rests?"

Paul continued his smirk and shrugged.

She pondered this suggestion. "But what if someone else comes along, drops in a quarter, and wins my millions?"

He didn't move or change his expression. "Don't you already have millions?"

She threw him a sideways glance, taking her eyes off of the pictures of fruit she had been so fixated on. "Well, you can never have enough millions." She looked back at the fruit, still contemplating the rest Paul had suggested.

Still calm, he commented, "Is that what would make you happy?"

Her gaze continued for a long moment before she turned her head to look him square in the eye. "I don't think it's any of your business what makes me happy." Paul didn't comment, and she turned her head back to the machine, this time dropping her gaze to pick a quarter up off the machine and hold it between her fingertips. He felt the moments tick by before she quietly spoke again, still looking at the quarter. "Besides, what makes you think I'm unhappy?"

Paul's stoic expression never changed. He wasn't the kind of guy that was intimidated by women like her. "Oh, I don't know. Maybe it's because you sit alone at a bar two nights a week while your husband is the life the party on the other side of the room. Maybe it's because the only time I've seen you smile is when you win a few measly quarters from a machine that you'd dropped ten times that amount into." He paused and watched her closely. "Maybe it's because I've never seen someone look so utterly alone in all my life."

More seconds ticked by, and he saw a tear escape her eye and roll slowly down her cheek. She continued to look down at the quarter before answering softly. "Is it that obvious?"

He knew she knew the answer, and he didn't respond.

Continuing to examine the quarter, she whispered again, "Things haven't turned out exactly as I'd hoped." More seconds ticked by and, as if snapping out of her thoughts, she quickly wiped the tear from her cheek and looked up at the man next to her. "But I don't suppose there's much I can do about that now, is there?"

His cool stare met her look of dismissal. "Isn't there?"

Her eyes held his and widened as they searched for answers. She felt a small jolt rush through her. "What are you suggesting?"

He didn't flinch but held her gaze with a cool calm that unnerved her. "I haven't suggested anything."

Her eyes held his as small jolt after small jolt continued to surge through her. "Well, that's probably a good thing." She looked down at the gold band on her left hand.

"What would you like me to suggest?"

Her eyes darted back up to his. Suddenly, she knew what she wanted, but she was not about to get it from some overconfident waiter. Her eyes glanced down at his lips and then moved back up to his eyes as she felt a pull. "I – I don't know what I want," she lied.

He pursed his lips tightly. She had more resolve than he'd given her credit for. "Well," he broke her gaze and dismissively slapped a hand on the wooden bar he'd been leaning on before turning his head back to her, "let me know if you figure it out." He smiled a confident smile. "Good night, Mrs. Fairfield." He gave the bar two more light slaps and turned and walked into the crowd.

CHAPTER 11

"So did you marry your first love and live happily ever after?" Kylie asked, guessing an obvious finish to Madeline's story.

"No," the old woman shook her head. She smiled conspiratorially at the cupcake-maker next to her. "It was a secret love."

Now Kylie was intrigued. "Why was it a secret?"

The woman's eyes darkened again, losing the twinkle. "My father wouldn't allow it." She looked down at the puppy curled in her lap as she stroked the shiny black head. "I'll never forgive him for that," she mumbled almost to herself.

"Because of money?" Kylie guessed another obvious answer.

Madeline shook her head. "Because of who he associated with."

"His friends?"

"His employers."

Kylie was confused now. "So he worked at the Club, and that was bad because...?"

The old woman let out a slow sigh. "I should probably start from the beginning." She continued to stroke the dog's head, but Kylie could tell that her mind was no longer on the dog. "Willy and I were high school sweethearts." She smiled as she remembered. "I moved here at the end of the school year when I was fifteen. Willy and I knew we were soul mates on my first day of school when we set eyes on each other."

"You met your soul mate when you were only fifteen?" Kylie interrupted.

Madeline smiled and nodded as she continued to stare into her past life. "When I saw him, I knew how my life was going to be. I just knew. We were inseparable."

"So what happened?"

Her eyes darkened again. "In 1930, Detroit and most of

Michigan was run by The Purple Gang."

"Yeah, I heard they owned my house when it was a club," Kylie interrupted.

Madeline nodded. "We moved here from Detroit because that spring my Uncle Buckley had been shot by the gang in broad daylight in a hotel lobby in downtown Detroit."

Kylie sat quietly, a surprised expression on her face.

"My father worried for the family's safety and moved us to this remote location, hoping to escape the power of the gang and the violence that seemed to follow them." She looked at Kylie. "We'd lived here two months when my father heard that the gang operated Club Manitou. We were all forbidden from going near it or communicating with anyone associated with it."

"So did they kill Willy?" Kylie asked, again trying to shortcut the story.

Madeline smiled and shook her head. "No, just my heart."

Kylie heard the sadness in the woman's voice. "So tell me

what happened."

"When school let out for my sixteenth summer, Willy got a job as a runner." She looked at the young woman and broke the word down, "Kind of like an errand boy at the club." Her gaze moved to the puppy in her lap again. "He did whatever they wanted whenever they wanted, and he was handsomely rewarded for it."

"So how did your father find out?" Kylie interrupted.

"This is a small town. There aren't a lot of secrets in it." She let out a slow breath. "So my father forbade me to see Willy ever again." A heavy sadness fell over the room. "I'll never forgive him for that," she repeated.

Kylie felt a little disappointed. "So that's the end of the story? You just never saw your soul mate again?"

Madeline shook her head. "You can't keep soul mates apart." Her eyes twinkled. "We met in secret that summer," she smiled to herself at the memory. "We were crazy in love, and it was like a drug that I would beg, lie, or steal to get."

Kylie felt a small pang of jealousy. Had she ever felt that kind of love?

"We both had bicycles and, as you know, the club was filled with secret rooms, passages, and entrances and exits, so secretly meeting was not as hard as you would think." She looked at Kylie with knowing smile. "We didn't have cell phones back then, you know."

Kylie's mind was stuck on the "secret" portion of the story, but she didn't want to interrupt to ask about it. "So what happened?"

Madeline's face grew sad again. "As two teenagers, we had as much privacy as we wanted, thanks to the club." She threw a sharp glance at Kylie, "If you know what I mean."

Kylie smiled and blushed at the insinuation.

Another sigh came out of the old woman. "Anyway, by the end of the summer, I was expecting, and my father was just furious when he found out."

"I can imagine," Kylie whispered sympathetically, completely caught up in the story. "So what happened?"

"He shipped me off to Wisconsin to stay with a cousin and deliver the baby."

"So you have a child?"

Madeline shook her head. "She was adopted by a friend of my cousin's family in Wisconsin." She smiled weakly. "It was a very good home."

"So then you came home and you and Willy were together again?"

Again the woman shook her head. "My father knew he wouldn't be able to keep us apart. I finished school in Wisconsin. My father put me into secretarial school after that, and it was years before I could return to look for Willy."

"So did you find him?"

Madeline shook her head again. "By then, things had changed. Prohibition had ended. The club was still thriving, but gambling became its predominant evil. While I was gone, Willy had been promoted to a different club in Virginia."

"So did you go look for him there?" Kylie pushed.

Madeline looked at her new friend. "My father somehow convinced Willy's family to completely shun me." She was shaking her head in disbelief. "They wouldn't speak to me, and they wouldn't even walk on the same side of the street if they saw me."

"But surely someone at the club could tell you where he was."

"As I said, things had changed. The staff at the club had come and gone, and even the man Willy assisted, Paul Preston, had mysteriously disappeared." She shook her head. "Folks at the club were very tight-lipped with the locals. We weren't even allowed inside if we didn't work there." Her eyes narrowed as she looked at the woman seated next to her. "Be careful. Nothing good has ever happened at that place."

That statement startled Kylie. "What? So are you saying it's jinxed or haunted or something?"

The woman appeared exhausted by sharing her lengthy story. "I wouldn't know what to call it other than, despite all of the gambling that took place there, I certainly wouldn't call it lucky."

CHAPTER 12

Kylie let out a groan as she pulled the heavy pink carpet off of the tack strips that lined the large living room in her home. Dropping the latest section, she looked at her red hands, made a fist with one, and then opened it. "My hands are losing their strength," she mumbled to herself.

Cupcake yipped at her from atop a large section of rolled carpet.

"Oh, yeah, you think this is pretty fun, don't you?"

The puppy yipped again from her puppy mountain and wagged her tail.

Kylie walked to the edge of the newly-detached carpet section and began to roll. As she passed the living room closet, the carpet caught. She walked over and opened the closet door. "You've got to be kidding me," she complained to herself. "They even put the pink carpet in the closet."

She fished the hammer out of the long pocket in her

painter's pants and hooked it on the edge of the carpet to pull it up. Freeing it, she grasped the edge and pulled the piece out of the closet, popping sounds following her as it detached from the nails in the tack strip.

Stepping back into the closet, she grasped the edge of the carpet pad and pulled that back, too.

"What the...?" she wondered to herself as she noticed the floor of the closet didn't match the strips of hardwood covering the rest of the living room. Instead, it was one dark panel. She looked up and tugged the string hanging from a ceiling lightbulb.

Cupcake stood next to her owner, trying to see what was so interesting.

"It looks like we've found one of the secrets of the house that Madeline spoke about," Kylie smiled.

Hooking her hand under the inset handle, she lifted the lid of the trapdoor, and she and Cupcake leaned forward to gaze down into it.

"You stay back," she instructed the puppy. "We don't need you falling into anything else. She used an arm to scoot the puppy back before reaching down into the black pit to feel around for steps. Feeling none, she stuck her face into the hole, looking for something to step on. The weak ceiling bulb barely illuminated the closet and didn't cast its light far into the hole at all. She leaned back and patted the pockets of her overalls in search of her cell phone but found them empty.

"Hmm," she said, swinging her legs around her body and dropping them into the pit. "Surely there is something to step on down there." She scooted her butt closer and closer to the edge as her legs moved in further and further in a circling motion as they searched for something to step on. She'd just reached as far as she could go when one of her hands landed on the tack strip. "Ow!" she jolted, trying to step on something with her feet and sliding quickly through the trapdoor. Desperately reaching across the floor for something to grab on to, her arm landed on another tack strip and slid across it as she lost more ground.

As panic and pain set in, her legs flailed wildly below her, searching for something to step onto. Above the hole, only her shoulders remained visible as her bleeding forearms lay next to the very edge holding her up. She was surrounded by tack strips on every side.

Cupcake began to bark.

"Cupcakie," Kylie said weakly as she tried to hoist herself up but couldn't get enough leverage in the tight space to do so, "if you have any Lassie in you, now would be a good time to find it."

There was a loud knock at the door, and Cupcake left her owner and ran yipping to see who had arrived.

Kylie heard a man's voice. "Well, hi there, Cupcake. Is your mom home?"

Cupcake stood yipping as if her life depended on it.

Recognizing the voice, Kylie struggled desperately to push herself up from the pit, but she just couldn't get any leverage with the tack strips so close.

"Hello?" she heard him call.

She rolled her eyes in defeat. She was going to have to swallow her pride, but this was getting ridiculous. "Come on in."

Chief Lange stepped into the home and picked up the yipping puppy, who didn't stop. He looked around at the room of half-rolled carpeting and then behind him, into the kitchen. Finally he asked, "Where are you?"

Kylie tried one more time to hoist herself from the hole before admitting defeat. If only she could casually walk out of the closet as if nothing had happened. If only she didn't need his help yet again. "Grrrrah!" she let out a moan as her effort failed.

The chief followed the sound to the closet, but Kylie was surprised when he didn't swoop down and pull her up. "Whatcha doing?" he asked, looking at her calmly.

Kylie looked up at him unhappily. "Oh, just hanging around."

He smirked. "Do you need some help?"

"No, no," Kylie held up a hand as her elbows held on for dear life. "I've got this."

He calmly stroked the now-silent puppy's head. "I can tell. Are your arms getting tired?"

Kylie winced. "Yeah, kind of."

"Because I could pull you up."

"No, no, I've got this." She lifted her fingertips to wave him away dismissively.

He nodded calmly again. "You know your arms are bleeding."

She looked down at the punctures in her forearm and hand. "Yeah. Stupid tack strip."

He stood where he was. "Because I could put the dog down and, I don't know," his eyes wandered as if searching for the right words, "pull you up."

"No," Kylie responded firmly. "I don't need you to keep

showing up in your," she waved a finger at his navy blue outfit he often wore, "hunky firefighter outfit and rescuing me all the time."

He shrugged. "Okay, suit yourself." He leaned forward and kissed Cupcake's head before looking back up at Kylie. "So you think my outfit is hunky?"

Kylie rolled her eyes, unhappy she'd given him a compliment that would show that she'd noticed his outfit. Her muscles were trembling now as she fought to hold on.

Chief Lange looked down at the puppy. "I don't know, Cupcake, maybe this would be a good time to take you for a walk." The puppy recognized the word and yipped her agreement. Chief Lange looked back at Kylie. "Your mom seems a little hung up."

"Ha, ha," Kylie retorted. Her mind was flying through her options, but she wasn't coming up with any. "I've had a lot of cupcakes this week, I'd probably be too heavy for you to pull up," she made the excuse as she looked at his muscular arms that told her otherwise.

He nodded his head in mock agreement. "You're probably right. I could run home and get my ladder," he offered.

Kylie was starting to feel sick as her muscles grew weaker and weaker and her shoulders began to throb their protest. "You don't have it in your truck?"

"Nope," he calmly responded, looking down to the stroke Cupcake's sleek fur of her back. More minutes ticked by, and he glanced at his watch. "Your shoulders must be really hurting by now."

"It's like child birth," Kylie said through clenched teeth, holding back both tears and her pride.

"You know, no one has to know if you just let me pull you up."

"I don't want you to think I need you to go around rescuing me all the time."

"I won't think that," he assured.

"How else could you think of it?" she asked, a tear now

escaping her eye as she realized she was going to have to concede.

"I could think of it as prepayment for cupcakes."

"Oh, that's a good one," she squeaked out as the pain became unbearable and the blood from her wounds began to pool. "That's a really good one."

"Okay?"

"Okay, pull me up."

Without wasting another second, the firefighter set Cupcake down, straddled the hole in his hard-soled work boots, and placed a hand under each of her shoulders. "I've got you," he assured her as he easily hoisted her from the opening and set her on the floor.

Kylie collapsed from her feet onto her back, hugging her strained arms to her. "Oh, thank you, thank you, thank you," she moaned as she pulled herself into a fetal position.

"I've got a first aid kit in the truck," he told her as he left her and returned with a white metal box.

"Here, give me your arm." Cupcake sat protectively near Kylie's head as the chief cleaned her puncture wounds and bandaged up her arms. "So what's your opposition to being rescued?" he asked casually, keeping his focus on her wounds.

She shrugged sullenly. "I'm not necessarily opposed to it if it's, like, once a year." He didn't comment, so she continued. "But, among me, Cupcake, and Aunt Judy, you've been rescuing us a lot lately." He nodded but kept his focus on her wounds, so she continued on defensively. "And it just gets," she thought for the right word before finishing, "embarrassing."

"There's nothing wrong with accepting help from people," he informed her as he leaned back to inspect his handiwork."

"But not all the time," she defended. There was a short silence as she examined her bandages before she looked up at him sitting cross-legged next to her. "What are you doing here anyway?"

"Your Aunt Judy told me you were tearing out carpet, and I

thought you might need a truck to haul it away with."

"Oh." Kylie looked back at her wounds. "That was really nice," she said quietly.

"Technically," he told her, "it wouldn't have been a rescue unless you think carpet can be rescued."

She looked at the dirty pink carpet she was laying on. "Not this carpet."

He smiled. "Do you think you can sit up?"

Kylie used a sore shoulder to push herself up, and his hand moved to her back to assist her. "No more childbirth pains?"

Kylie threw him an irritated look. Maybe she had been a little dramatic.

Chuckling at his comment, he stood and walked over to the hole in the floor. "So what did you find?"

Distracted, Kylie forgot her pain and stepped next to him as they both gazed down the hole. "Some kind of trapdoor. Too bad you don't have your ladder."

He slipped his hands casually into the front pockets of his navy blue Dickies and jingled some change before looking at her. "You know, we could just go down into the basement and see where it comes out."

Kylie looked and him and blushed before shrugging and saying as if she was making some sort of compromise, "Or we could do it that way."

CHAPTER 13

Phyllis watched Paul from across the room. He hadn't spoken to her since their last conversation. Weeks had passed and, the more time that passed, the more she thought about him. She craned her neck to see into the gambling room and spotted her husband throwing his head back in laughter at the Roulette table.

She was taking another sip from her tea cup of gin when she saw Paul beckon to the bartender, drawing him to the far end of the bar. They stood closely and spoke, the bartender's back to her. She squinted her eyes, trying to read their lips, but it was a futile effort. Paul's eyes caught her intent gaze, and she threw him a smile that was probably too large to appear anything but desperate. He didn't return it.

Frustrated, she put her drink down and walked to the end of the bar, positioning herself behind Paul. When his conversation finished, he turned, and she was inches from his face. The two held eye contact as seconds ticked by with tiny jolts coursing through her body, reminding Phyllis of what she was feeling. Finally, she said it.

"I know what I want."

He held his close ground. "And what's that, Mrs. Fairfield? Another drink?"

The hurt caused by his comment showed in her eyes, and he immediately regretted saying it.

"Can I talk to you," her eyes darted side to side to make sure no one was listening before she continued, "alone?"

He didn't look away from her before responding, "This is a busy night. The only spot you're going to get away from two hundred people would be in a bathroom." He didn't offer her any of the spots on the second floor.

She swallowed and nodded, lifting her chin defiantly. "Very well then." She held his eye contact for a moment as she carefully stepped away from him and began to cross the room.

Paul stood at the bar, watching her. His jaw tightened when he saw her approach the ladies room, place her hand on the doorknob, and then turn to look back at him. He watched her step inside. He hesitated only a moment to look around to see if anyone else was watching before he began a slow walk across the room, his right hand casually pressing straight the front of his white dinner jacket. He approached the wait station next to the door, leaned to pick up the plunger on the floor next to it, casually walked to the ladies room door, and slipped inside.

Phyllis stood with her hands behind her, resting nervously against the sink. She watched Paul lock the door behind himself and set the plunger down. He didn't say a word as he approached her, ending his short walk to stand dangerously close to her.

Phyllis met his eye contact, again feeling the tiny jolts coursing through her and awakening parts of her she didn't know existed. "I know what I want," she repeated to him.

He didn't budge. "And what's that, Mrs. Fairfield?"

She felt the tension growing the longer she waited in silence, their bodies only inches apart. "I want it all." She rose to her tiptoes, wrapped her right hand behind his neck, and urgently pulled her lips to his. It was a long, slow kiss that would forever change their futures.

Paul studied her face when it ended.

She searched his eyes for anything, but he was a hard man to read. "I know there will be consequences, but this is what I want," she quietly assured him.

Paul only hesitated seconds to digest this final statement before hungrily pulling her lips to his and lifting her onto the edge of the sink.

CHAPTER 14

Chief Lange's flashlight shined up to the hole in the ceiling of Kylie's basement.

Her gaze followed the light, and she leaned her head close to his so she would see what he saw. "I don't see anything except an extra board there," she confessed after a few seconds had passed with him shining his light into several different areas.

"Hmm, he commented as he shined his light across the room to the stairs that led outside.

"'Hmm' what?"

"Well, that extra board," he shined his flashlight on it as he spoke, "is a brace. You can see the small hinges left on the sides there. I suspect there was a collapsible ladder attached to it at one time."

"Why wouldn't they just take the stairs?" Kylie asked.

The chief looked behind him at the incinerator and then back up at the hole. "My guess is they never really used the ladder though. My guess is, during a raid, they would drop incriminating documents through the trap door to be placed into the incinerator."

"Ooh, that's a good idea," Kylie approved.

He ignored her and continued on. "This concrete door here and the sliding steel door at the base of the stairs would both be closed to hold the authorities off until the incriminating evidence could be destroyed."

Kylie looked at the doors, blinking and taking it in.

"The doors wouldn't hold the authorities out forever, but it would be long enough to destroy evidence."

"Like chips?"

"Chips, score cards, tally sheets, bodies" he turned his gaze to her, "you name it."

"Bodies?" She hoped he was joking.

He nodded towards the incinerator. "Have you looked in

there yet?"

"Um, no. Why would I?" She was starting to see a pattern forming as the Chief was the second man to ask her if she'd looked in something she owned.

He stepped over the cement block laying on the floor, once used to conceal the door opening, and opened the small fourteen-by-fourteen-inch door of the nearly hundred-year-old incinerator. "To see if anything is left inside."

"Oh, good idea," Kylie stuck her face next to his to gaze inside the soot-covered cavern. "You were kidding about the bodies part, right?"

Ignoring her comment, Chief Lange stepped back, picked up a long, soot-covered bar from the floor, and began to pull the ashes towards the opening with the rod. He reached inside and pulled out a corner of a piece of paper and blew the soot off.

"What's it say?" Kylie asked, leaning in to try to discern the handwriting.

"Not enough to make out any full words." He set the scrap of paper on top of the incinerator and closed its door. Shining his flashlight along the walls, he asked, "Did you ever find the origination point of that air shaft that Cupcake fell into?"

Kylie blushed. "I forgot all about it."

She and Cupcake followed Chief Lange along the entire perimeter of the basement as he shined his flashlight along the cement block wall and then the paneled walls of the main room. She was impressed with his quiet patience as he finished the loop back in the incinerator room, where his eyes rested on the large safe.

"I looked in that," Kylie reported proudly. "There's nothing in it."

He shot her a look as his flashlight remained on the safe. "But did you look behind it?"

Kylie pursed her lips but didn't say anything as the chief stepped to the safe and shined his light behind it.

"Ah-ha!" he let out a triumphant exclamation that brought Cupcake scampering to his side. He sat his flashlight on top, wrapped his strong fingers around the edge of the four-foot-tall safe, and pulled it inches from the wall to expose a three-and-a-half foot square tunnel.

Kylie let out a gasp.

"Here we have an air shaft, folks," he announced.

Cupcake ran forward to try to enter it, but Kylie grabbed her and scooped her up. "Don't you even think about it, Cupcakie. Air vents are off limits to you."

Cupcake licked Kylie's cheek with her sandpapery tongue.

"So we found it. Mystery solved," Kylie announced with a clap of her hands.

The chief stood up and put his hands on his hips, still staring at the tunnel. "We just have one problem."

The joy left Kylie's face. "Oh, no. What?"

"This isn't the air shaft Cupcake fell into."

"How do you know?"

"This tunnel exits the back of the building, but you can see," he shined his light inside, "it sharply turns right and heads east."

"The one Cupcake fell into is to the west," Kylie realized aloud.

He nodded his head in agreement.

"Could it curve around?"

"Not likely."

"So where does this one lead to?"

He leaned on the cement wall with one hand and casually crossed one leg in front of the other. "The way I see it, we have three options."

"Three?"

"First, we can hook a GoPro camera onto Cupcake and send her in."

Kylie squeezed her puppy safely to her before giving the chief a firm, "No."

He chuckled. "I didn't think that one would fly."

"What's the next option?"

"The next option is we walk around outside and see if we can find it to the east of the building."

"That might be difficult if no one has found it before."

"Yep. That's option two."

"What's option three?"

"We walk through it ourselves and see where it comes out."

"Uh, you mean crawl. No, thanks."

He handed her the flashlight. "Take a closer look."

Confused, Kylie took the flashlight in exchange for Cupcake. Stepping closer, she shined it into the three and a half foot high square.

"Kneel down," he instructed.

She took a quick glance at him before kneeling and placing a hand inside the square opening.

"Shine the light up."

As the light spread to a larger area, Kylie drew in a gasp. "It's a tunnel!" Without thinking, she started to crawl past the two-foot long vent portion to reach the standing area when something grabbed her ankle and pulled her back. "Hey!" she protested.

"I think you should let me go first."

Remaining on her knees, she protested. "It's my house, I can go first. I don't think there's anything I need you to rescue me from in there."

"Could be wild animals if the other end is open."

Kylie glanced back at the opening. In her excitement, she hadn't thought of any dangerous possibilities.

"It's old. It could also be unstable."

Kylie tightened her lips together before moving over to let him through.

Handing her the puppy, he dropped to all fours. "Hand her to me when I stand up."

Kylie did as she was instructed and, after crawling the two feet, stood up in an arched tunnel lined from floor to ceiling in cobblestones. "Cool!" she whispered.

Chief Lange was shining his light along the ceiling ahead. "There are roots hanging down from the top. I'd question its stability considering its age."

"This matches the exterior entrance to the basement," Kylie pointed out, running her fingertips over the damp cobblestones.

"They must have all been built originally. Some were hidden, and some were used regularly."

Kylie grabbed Cupcake from the chief. "Let's go!"

CHAPTER 15

"This way, Maddie," Willy instructed after they left their bikes behind a large tree on the circle drive of Club Manitou.

"Wait," she pleaded, unsure of her footing in the summer dusk.

Willy ran back to her, giving her cheek a gentle peck before grabbing her hand to guide her.

"Are you sure we won't get in trouble?" she asked, gazing at the prestigious dinner club with windows aglow with warm light and music seeping out of its every crack.

"Positive. I work here. They know me," he assured.

Maddie let him guide her to the large garage located some distance from the club. Just like the club, it was constructed in a large log cabin style, white mortar filling the space between the dark logs. The building sat dark and lonely in comparison to the lively club nearby where Maddie could hear voices and laughter intertwined with the music.

"Do you think someday we'll be able to go in there like everyone else?" she asked her companion.

Willy hesitated and followed her gaze before opening the garage door. "Mr. Gerhart doesn't allow locals. Only summer folk."

"Why is that?" Maddie wondered.

"The summer folk are the ones with the money." He leaned on the door frame and shook his head to indicate how impressed he was. "Things sure are fancy in there, Maddie."

"What's so fancy?"

Willy smiled. "They have live lobsters brought in by train every week."

"Live?"

He nodded. "Real linen tablecloths on every table, even in the basement." His eyes appeared dreamy. "The thickest steaks you've ever seen. Bands are playing every night, and the cupboards are stocked with more liquor than you could ever imagine."

Maddie's eyes were dreamy. "And the women, what do the women wear?"

Willy smirked. "Oh, fine furs, even in the summertime, and the latest dresses from New York City. The men all have the best cars from Detroit."

Maddie watched the warm yellow glow coming from every window and felt like she was missing out.

Willy tugged her hand again. "Come on, we'll get closer."

Hesitant to look away from the sight before her, Willy's second tug pulled her through the side door of the garage.

Stepping inside, Willy easily lit a lantern near the door that filled the room with light.

"Don't they have electric lights in here?" Maddie wondered.

"Yeah, but not where we're going."

Maddie's eyes widened as Willy led her across the room to a large, built-in tool cabinet.

"Here, hold this," Willy instructed as he opened the double doors and lifted the two empty center shelves out, placing them on top of other shelves. Leaning into the opening, he pulled open a trapdoor in the bottom of it, revealing a round hole going below."

"Wow," Maddie whispered in awe.

Proud to be the one impressing her, Willy beamed as he held out his hand for the lantern. "Hang on to the rail, Maddie. The steps get wet." Without another thought, he disappeared down the steps and into the hole.

Maddie looked around the large garage to see if anyone was watching before following Willy into the ground.

"Can you shine the light up so I can see?" she begged, suddenly afraid.

Willy lifted the lamp from the bottom of the spiral staircase that he had quickly descended. "Go slow, Maddie. I'll wait."

Knuckles gripping the rail tightly, Maddie wound her way to the bottom of the stairwell, stepping onto a floor of square cobblestones before taking Willy's hand again.

"Check it out, Maddie," Willy said proudly as he held up the lantern to reveal a long, arched tunnel covered from floor to ceiling with smooth cobblestones. "Neat, huh?"

"Neat," she agreed, impressed.

"Come on!" he urged as his hand tugged hers ahead through the dark tunnel towards the club.

After two hundred yards, Maddie slowed her walk. "It ends, Willy. How do we get in?"

Willy grinned. "This is the really neat part."

Setting the lantern on the floor, he got down on all fours. "We have to put out the lantern now," he instructed.

Maddie wasn't entirely comfortable with that but did as she was told before dropping to all fours next to Willy.

"Leave the lantern here. We'll get it on the way back."

Crawling into a three and a half foot wide square duct, Willy reached ahead and pulled open the end of it, revealing a screened window with busy legs moving by it. Music streamed into the tunnel along with raucous laughter and, closer by, people speaking.

"Where are we?" Maddie whispered to Willy.

"We're in the kitchen," he informed. "We're hidden behind a rolling set of shelves." He pointed his finger kitty-corner across the room. "See that little square in the cement wall?"

Maddie nodded.

"That's where they get rid of everything when there's a raid."

"Then they run out through this tunnel and get away?" she whispered.

He nodded. "Or one of the others."

She looked at him with surprise. "'Others'?" she repeated. "There's more?"

He grinned a dimpled grin at her. "Yep, and hidden rooms

and trap doors and moving walls on the bandstand. It's just like in the movies."

Maddie watched the people she could see from the waist down bustling back and forth in front of them. Voices intermingled with the music and laughter. There was the occasional whirring of the Roulette table and intermittent dings from the slot machines. An authoritative voice interrupted the garbled ones, and she saw creased black pants and shiny shoes step in front of her.

"I'll be upstairs for a while, fellas. If anyone needs me, don't come looking."

Maddie saw the man with the authoritative voice lift the bottom of his white dinner jacket and slip a champagne flute into each front pocket of his pants while the other men in the kitchen laughed.

"That's my boss," Willy informed her in the quietest of whispers. "Mr. Preston."

As the man turned to leave, Maddie saw him swing a

champagne bottle off of the countertop, momentarily swinging it by his thigh before slipping it inside his jacket and pulling it closed. After he'd stepped away, Maddie asked, "What's upstairs?"

Willy threw her another dimpled grin. "Staff living quarters," he said with a wink that made Maddie blush and look away.

CHAPTER 16

Phyllis rolled away and reached for the champagne flute on the nightstand as Paul lay on his back, taking a slow draw from his cigarette. "This certainly is a step up from the bathroom," she commented dryly as she sipped.

"I prefer to stay closer to your husband in case he comes looking for you."

Phyllis set her glass back down and rolled to her opposite side, propping her head up on a pillow with her hand. "He hasn't come looking all summer."

Paul tapped his cigarette on the ashtray. "One thing I know is to never get too comfortable."

Phyllis watched him closely. "Would it be so bad if we got caught?"

He turned his head to look at her. "Is that what you want?"

She shrugged. "Maybe he won't mind."

Paul didn't react.

"Maybe it would be easier."

"Could you go back home?" he asked, careful not to make her any offers or promises.

She reached her left arm over and curled some of the hair on his chest around the tip of a finger. "I don't think so."

Paul remained silent, knowing her other option.

She continued to focus on his chest hair. "Change is scary, you know."

"But you're comfortable with the way things are now?"

She smiled the slightest bit, still staring at his chest. "It's kind of exciting."

Paul took another draw on his cigarette, and she took it from him, doing the same before she returned it to him.

The small smile was still there while she exhaled before she spoke again. "I go through every day waiting for Henry to suggest we come to the club for dinner."

"And the days you don't?"

Her eyes saddened again and met his. "Those are the worst days."

"You don't need me, you know. You're a Whitley; you can do anything you want."

Holding his eye contact, she gave her head the slightest shake. "Henry controls everything."

"But your family?"

"Daddy would disown me and write me out of his will if I left Henry." She reached for the cigarette and took another draw. "I've been Daddy's plan for Henry since I was born."

His jaw tightened. "So you never loved him?"

She exhaled slowly. "I don't believe in love."

Paul had an amused look in his eyes as he turned to put out the cigarette. "Good thinking. It only gets in the way."

Her hand returned to his body as she asked, "And what about you? You aren't married, are you?"

Paul slipped a hand on top of hers. "No. I don't believe in marriage."

She nodded in acknowledgment. "Oh, to be a man and be able to choose." She intertwined her fingers with his. "And love? Have you ever been in love?"

Paul shook his head. "I never had time to think about it."

She nodded again, smoothly running her fingers back and forth against his. "And what about work?"

Paul felt defensive. "What about work?"

"Have you always wanted to be a waiter? Don't you want more?" Her tone was condescending.

He smirked in relief. He'd let her assume what she wanted. "I've always wanted to be in the family business," he answered vaguely.

"And your family has a restaurant?"

He nodded honestly, lifting her hand to his mouth to kiss it. "Something like that." He rolled onto his side to face her, propping his head up on a hand as she was. "And what about you? Did you ever want to be anything besides a wife?"

She touched his chest again, focusing on it to avoid eye contact. "I never wanted to be a wife."

He slipped a finger under her chin and lifted her eyes to his. "So what did you want?"

"Why does my heart nearly stop every time I look into your eyes?" she asked, avoiding a direct response to his question.

He didn't answer.

"I feel sweaty and nervous and sick," she paused before continuing, "but I don't want to stop looking at you. It's like some kind of drug." Still holding her chin, he leaned in and kissed her softly before pulling back again. "I think you're what I wanted," she whispered.

His hand lingered on her chin, but he didn't break her gaze. "You don't love me." He watched for a change in her expression. Seeing none, he continued, "You don't even know me."

She forced a small smile in an effort to ease the tension. "I know you enough. I know you're not some murderer or bandit or something."

He didn't look away from her gaze. "Aren't I?"

She looked uncomfortable for the first time. "No, you're not."

"What if I were? Would that change things?"

She wriggled to get away from his intense gaze, but his hand held her chin firmly in place so her eyes couldn't leave his. Forced to look into his eyes, she hesitated and then came to terms with herself. "I suppose it wouldn't."

Paul searched her eyes to try to read how much she actually understood. He was met by a calm gaze that matched his own when he knew he had a job to do. Pulling her mouth to his, he kissed her again, this time lingering. "I should get you back downstairs," he whispered.

"Yes, you should," she agreed as her leg moved on top of his and up to his thigh before wrapping around his buttocks and pulling him to her. "I'll just need another minute of your time first."

CHAPTER 17

"Are you sure this is solid?" Kylie asked as she followed Chief Lange into the tunnel of crumbling cobblestone, clutching Cupcake under an arm. "This has got to be a hundred years old."

"Nope," the chief answered as he took slow steps ahead, his flashlight illuminating the path.

With every step they took, small amounts of dirt fell from the ceiling. Kylie grabbed onto the back of his shirt and clutched it as she followed. "That's not the answer I was hoping for."

Without changing his focus from the tunnel, his free hand moved back and removed hers from his shirt, grasping it in his.

Surprised, Kylie hesitated before softly wrapping her fingertips around his large hand.

"I wouldn't want you to wrinkle my hunky outfit," he commented casually, still focusing on the tunnel in front of them.

Kylie gasped and tried to pull her hand from his, but he held on.

"It's this or nothing."

She thought a moment before conceding. "So how far do you think this goes?" she asked, trying to steer the conversation away from the handholding.

"To right about there."

Kylie poked her head to the side of his arm to see a metal spiral staircase illuminated ahead of them. "I'm trying to think where on the property we are now," she mused at the staircase. "We're definitely well outside of the house."

"Northeast corner of the property," he commented as he used his flashlight to inspect the base and overall structure of the stairwell.

"The garage," she mumbled.

"It makes for the perfect getaway." He gave the spiral staircase a good shake to ensure its stability before he started up.

"Yeah," she agreed, her eyes following the light he shined down for her to illuminate the first step. Something glared back at her from the crumbling mortar between cobblestones. "Wait. What's that?"-

"What's what?"

"There's something shiny in the corner behind the stairs."

The chief flashed his light along the perimeter until it reflected on something. Dropping his hand, Kylie handed off Cupcake as she squeezed behind the handrail at the base of the stairs in the tight tunnel. Crouching, she ran her hands over the damp stones until her fingertips found the thin chain. "Got it!" she exclaimed loudly, jumping up. Her voice echoed throughout the tunnel, and dirt fell again.

"Good. Let's get out of here," the chief suggested. "I wouldn't come down here again without my hard hat."

Grabbing her hand again to keep her close, Chief Lange continued up the metal spiral steps that squeaked painfully with each step that they held. Reaching the top, the chief tapped on the ceiling with his flashlight, and it seemed to give. "Hold this," he instructed, dropping her hand to give her the flashlight.

Kylie shined the light at the ceiling as the chief placed both of his large hands above and pushed. The ceiling easily lifted in the shape of a square about three feet and then stopped.

"It's another trapdoor," Kylie announced.

"And something is above it," the chief retorted. "Take a couple steps down. This is going to take some force."

Kylie gripped Cupcake tightly before dropping back a couple steps. The chief let the door drop closed before giving it a hard heave. She heard more dirt fall from the ceiling below as the door flew open and a board fell in.

"Watch out!" he called as he stepped back and Kylie saw the falling board coming straight at her.

CHAPTER 18

Maddie and Willy sat holding hands on the hillside above one of the tunnel openings. Their eyes focused on a stream of exhaust left by one of the airplanes that had just taken off. In front of them, they could see the blue waters of Little Traverse Bay and, beyond that, the City of Petoskey extending up the hillside on the opposite side.

She leaned and snuggled her head into his shoulder. "What are we going to do?"

"I can't quit my job, Maddie. I'll never find another job that pays this much."

"I know," she sighed, staring ahead. "Maybe you could get a second job and just tell Daddy you quit."

"Maddie, there aren't a lot of jobs around here for a sixteen-year-old kid."

She nodded, knowing he was right.

"We'll just have to keep things a secret until I save enough for us to get married."

"Married?" she lifted her head and looked at him in surprise. "But we're only sixteen."

Willy shrugged his shoulders. "That's the only way I can see your father would let us be together."

"He wouldn't approve."

"Then we'll elope."

Maddie turned her body, leaving the view of the sparkling blue waters of the bay and focusing on her first love. "And do what, Willy? We can't live a life in hiding. How will we pay rent and buy food? We're still kids."

Willy pulled a tall piece of grass out and stuck the thick end between his teeth as he thought. "Mr. Preston has a lot of connections in Detroit. Maybe he can help me get a job there."

Maddie looked alarmed. "In the city? How will we get there?"

"Train."

Maddie's gaze dropped, and she thought a moment. "Do you think you can save that much by the end of the summer?"

He shrugged. "Maybe." He squinted into the sun as he chewed and thought. "Might have to wait until next season."

"Daddy would come after me," Maddie mused sadly.

Willy turned to face her now. "Maddie, Mr. Preston and Mr. Gerhart, they have connections. People they like, they protect."

Maddie pulled back a bit. "I don't want anything bad to happen to my family, Willy." She held up a palm to face him as was their habit, "I just want to be with you."

He placed his palm against hers, and their fingers bent to lock hands. "Me too, Maddie. Me too."

The sound of a seagull screeched overhead as their eyes held.

"I love you, Maddie. I'd do anything for you."

"I know." She leaned in and kissed him softly. "I never want to be apart, Willy. Never."

"I'd never let that happen, Maddie."

"Promise?"

He tightened the grip on her hand. "Always, Maddie. Always."

She leaned in to kiss him again, this time placing her free hand on the side of his face. His free arm wrapped around her and pulled her closer.

Her kisses moved from his lips to his cheek, down his neck, and to his ear where she gently tugged at his earlobe with her teeth. "Take me into the tunnel, Willy."

He pulled back in an effort to read her eyes. "Are you sure?"

Her hand gave his a squeeze, and she smiled shyly at him as she nodded. "Yes. Really sure."

Willy smiled, and the two young lovers stood and walked through the tall summer grass and down the hillside with interlocked hands towards the grate-covered opening below them.

CHAPTER 19

"Willy, I need you to do something for me," the man commanded in a steady voice, running a hand through his thick, dark hair.

"Yes, Mr. Preston, sir." Willy jumped up, ready to be at the beck and call of the quietly intimidating man who sat at the closed bar that afternoon, smoking a cigarette.

He took a draw on his cigarette and gave a nod towards one of the empty stools next to him at the bar. "Have a seat."

Thrilled to have his boss pay him this much attention, Willy slipped quickly onto the stool next to him.

"How do you like it here?"

"It's great, sir."

Paul exhaled. "The fellas treating you all right?"

"Yes, sir. Great."

Paul nodded and focused on putting his cigarette butt out in the ashtray. "I need you to do something for me."

"Yes, sir."

"It's just between you and me." He turned to look at the sixteen-year-old next to him. "I don't want anyone else knowing."

"Yes, sir."

Reluctant to let go of the butt, he continued. "We have a regular customer, Mr. Fairfield." He looked at the boy. "You know who I'm talking about?"

"Yes, I do, sir."

Paul released the butt and crossed his arms on the wooden bar. "Next time he comes in here, I want you to follow him when he leaves."

"Okay, sir." Willy sounded confused. "Did he do something wrong?"

Paul shook his head. "I don't know. I just want to know the full picture as far as what's going on."

Willy nodded.

Paul reached into his pocket and pulled out a wad of neatly-folded bills. He mindlessly peeled some of the bills off and held them up to Willy. "I want you to follow him until he returns here." He rubbed the bills together between his fingers. "It might be a few days."

"Yes, sir." Willy reached hungrily for the bills, but Paul pulled them away.

"Discretion. I want discretion. No one is to see you, and I don't want you telling anyone about this."

"Yes, sir," Willy agreed again. This time, Paul relaxed his arm and lowered the bills towards Willy, who eagerly snatched them from him. "Thank you, sir."

"You can go," the man dismissed as he looked down at his coffee cup and swirled the dark liquid inside.

Willy hesitated, and Paul looked back at his employee. "There will be more when you report back."

Willy looked down at the cash in his hand. "It's not that, sir." He thought carefully as he chose his words. "Mr. Preston, there's this girl."

Paul smirked and rolled his head to the side in understanding. "Oh, it's about a girl."

Willy nodded as he looked down, lacking the confidence to make eye contact and ask favors. "We want to elope, Mr. Preston, and I was wondering if you might be able to help me out with a job in Detroit."

Paul lost his smirk and squinted at the boy. "What are you? Eighteen?"

"Sixteen, sir," Willy responded nervously, still looking down at his lap.

Paul took a sip of his coffee. "Sixteen." He thought for a moment as Willy felt his nervousness grow. "What's your rush?"

Willy felt color flush his cheeks. "Her father doesn't want us to be together."

Paul nodded solemnly and focused on the stocked bar in front of him. "Because of your employment?"

More color flushed Willy's cheeks. "Yes, sir," came his mumbled reply.

Paul nodded again. "And you chose to stay on and risk losing your girl rather than get a job at the grocery store?"

Willy nodded again, still focusing on his lap.

Paul took another sip from the white coffee cup in front of him. "That's a sign of loyalty," he acknowledged. He looked at the boy. "Loyalty is the most important thing to me." Willy sat in insecure silence waiting for his answer. Paul gave his palm a light slap on the bar, drawing the boy's focus upwards. "Tell you what. Come the end of the summer season, we'll work something out."

Willy's face lit up. "Really, sir?"

Paul smiled one of his half smiles. "Keep up the good work, and we'll find something for you."

Willy rose from the stool, overjoyed. "Thank you, sir," he

nodded, getting ready to leave.

Paul focused on his coffee again. "Did you get her anything?"

Willy turned back. "Get her anything?"

"Yeah. Something to show your commitment." When he didn't get a response, he looked at the boy. "You know, a bracelet, necklace, ring. Anything like that?"

Willy blushed again. "No, sir. Just my word."

Paul took another sip and set the cup down. "A man's word is good, but you should always put down collateral."

"Collateral?" Willy wasn't familiar with the word.

He looked at the boy. "So she has something left if you leave."

"Oh, I'd never – "

"Never say never, boy," he interrupted, turning to him. "Things come up. You never know what could happen." His eyes scanned the walls of the basement speakeasy. "This isn't exactly the safest place to work." His eyes met those of the boy. "If something were to happen, you'd want her to know."

Willy swallowed hard hearing the safety information that he'd refused to acknowledge as true said aloud. "I'll take a look around town," he whispered and turned to leave.

"Wait." Paul fished out his stack of neatly-folded bills again and peeled off several. Holding them out to Willy, he said, "When you find your collateral, get two."

CHAPTER 20

Kylie awoke to the sounds of Chief Lange talking into his radio as she felt herself being jostled.

"Yes, a possible concussion. I'm pulling into Emergency right now."

Still groggy, she turned her head in an effort to take in her surroundings. "Ouch!" she exclaimed as she lifted a hand to her head. "Ouch!" she repeated when she felt pain in her arm.

Stopping his truck at the Emergency Room entrance, Chief Lange looked back. "Yeah, you got a pretty good knock on the head." He jumped out, ran around to the other side, and opened the back door of the pickup as two men with a stretcher came out of the hospital.

"Seriously? A stretcher?" Kylie asked with her hand still on her head.

"Just to be safe," the chief informed as he reached an arm up to help pull her out of the truck cab and onto the stretcher.

"You were in and out of consciousness for quite a while."

"This is so humiliating," she mumbled.

He smirked as he closed the door. "I'll park the truck and be right in."

"You don't have to stay," Kylie called from the stretcher. "I'm okay."

He smirked again. "Just to be safe."

Kylie rolled her eyes, frustrated.

The attendants rolled her straight to a room, and a nurse stepped in and immediately placed a clamp onto her finger.

"What's this for?" Kylie asked as the nurse began to wrap a blood pressure cuff around her arm.

"It checks the level of oxygen in your system."

"Hi, I'm Dr. Cole," a smart-looking thirty-something doctor introduced herself.

Kylie returned her handshake. "Hi."

"So what are you here for today?" the doctor questioned as she pushed her dark glasses further up on her nose.

"I got hit in the head, and the chief worried I might have a concussion," Kylie informed begrudgingly. "But I'm fine. I feel fine."

"That's great to hear, Miss," she looked down at the documents in front of her, "Branson. Why don't I just give you a quick check, and we'll try to get you on your way."

Kylie dropped her head back on the stretcher and nodded before lifting her hand to her aching head. Feeling something sticky, she pulled her hand away to look at the blood on it. "I might need stitches though."

The doctor stepped closer and lifted one of Kylie's arms to examine it. "And what happened here?"

Kylie blushed. "I got caught on some tack strip."

Dr. Cole scrunched her eyebrows together. "On the floor?"

"Er, yeah," Kylie replied in a tone that let the doctor know she didn't want to talk about it.

Dr. Cole leaned in to examine the cut on Kylie's head as she spoke. "So how are you feeling now? Dizzy? Nauseous? Headache?"

"Well, my head hurts where the cut is," Kylie grumbled.

"Okay," the doctor acknowledge, palpating the skin around the cut. "Anything else?"

Kylie rotated her shoulder to look at it. "Ugh, and I have this big bruise on my upper arm."

Dr. Cole nodded her acknowledgment before turning to the nurse. "We can get away with a butterfly bandage on her cut after it's cleaned."

She turned back to Kylie. "Do you remember what happened?"

Kylie thought a moment. "We were going up some stairs, and something fell and hit me."

"Do you know what it was?"

Kylie thought again and shook her head. "I don't remember."

"Did you fall down the stairs?"

Kylie chewed her lip for a moment as she tried to remember. "I don't know."

Dr. Cole nodded her acknowledgment and stepped closer. "Okay, just let me check out your eyes," she informed, pulling out an instrument with a light on it. "Look to the left." Kylie did so. "And now the right." Kylie let out a breath. "Uh-huh. Now follow my finger." The doctor moved her finger back and forth. "Good." She stepped back and pocketed the instrument. "I think you came out of this okay, but we're going to send you for a CAT scan just to be sure."

Kylie propped herself up on an elbow. "A CAT scan? How much will that cost?"

The doctor smiled in understanding. "Your insurance will

cover it after your copay."

Kylie let out a growl and dropped onto her back again.

There was a knock at the door, and Chief Lange poked his head around the corner. "Safe to come in?"

"Are you her husband?" Dr. Cole asked.

"No!" Kylie said emphatically as Chief Lange simultaneously gave the same answer in a calm tone.

The doctor smiled.

"I'm the one who brought her in," the chief told the doctor.

"Ah. Were you with her when this happened?"

"Yes."

"Did she fall down the stairs?"

"No," he glanced at Kylie, knowing she wouldn't like what he had to say, "I caught her."

Kylie rolled her eyes and moaned, "Nooooo."

He smiled.

"Did you see what hit her?"

He nodded. "It was a piece of shelving about this long." He held his hand apart to indicate about three feet in length.

The doctor nodded. "Sounds like she was lucky you were there."

"Maybe so," the chief acknowledged as the doctor stepped past him out of the room. He approached Kylie's bedside.

"Did you let Aunt Judy know?"

He nodded and sat in the chair next to her bed and crossed his arms. "So tell me, Miss Branson, what's your aversion to being rescued?"

Kylie rolled her eyes again and let out a grunt.

He smiled confidently at her. "Because you'd be surprised what catnip it is to some women when they hear I'm a firefighter."

The nurse flashed him a shy smile as she finished cleaning

Kylie's gash and placed a butterfly bandage onto it before leaving.

Kylie shot him an irritated glance before she answered. "I told you, it's just embarrassing. I'm not one of those girls that needs some handsome man to swoop in and rescue me all the time."

He remained calm with his arms crossed. "So you think I'm handsome, huh?"

"Ugh," she grunted again.

"Frankly," he lifted his eyebrows, "you look like you've just come back from war." Kylie looked at the bandages on her arms again as he spoke. "You could probably use more rescuing than I've been able to give you."

Kylie clenched her fists together next to her on the bed. "Well, just stop doing it."

He shrugged. "Okay."

"Just treat me like a normal person, not some damsel in distress."

He smirked at her, holding back a laugh in an effort to remain serious. "I'll make you a deal, you stop losing your dog, falling through holes, and getting hit by falling objects, and I'll stop rescuing you."

Kylie softened a bit. "I'm not normally like this," she informed. "I don't know what's wrong with me lately with all of this weird stuff happening." She lifted her arms to show him her bandages from the tack strip. "Look at me!"

As her arms lifted, something fell from her hand and caught her eye. "What's this?" Her mind fought to remember as she picked up a locket on a thin chain.

Chief Lange leaned forward, placing his elbows on his knees. "I think it's what you found in the tunnel before we started up the stairs. You must have been gripping it in your hand when you got hit."

Kylie picked up the delicate gold chain and tiny locket with flowers engraved on the front. "It's beautiful," she whispered.

Chief Lange got up and stepped to the bed to inspect it. "Open it."

Kylie glanced up at him before popping open the tiny circle. She pulled it closer to better see its contents, and Chief Lange leaned his head near to hers to equally get a better look. "It's a young woman," she looked to the other side of the circle, "and man."

The chief squinted his eyes at the tiny photos. "Any idea who they are?"

Kylie shook her head before turning it to look at the chief, his face only inches from hers. "No," she whispered, her eyes glancing down at his lips so close to her own before meeting his gaze again. "I have no idea."

CHAPTER 21

"It's beautiful," Phyllis gasped as she opened the box with the tiny gold locket inside, intricately engraved with flowers. Her dark eyes lifted sadly to Paul's. "But you know I can't wear it."

"Do you think he would even notice?" Paul commented, reluctant to speak Henry's name.

"I don't know," she said sadly looking back down at the locket.

"He doesn't have to know it's a locket," Paul suggested. "Just tell him you bought it for yourself."

"Maybe," she shrugged.

"Open it." Phyllis opened the locket to find a tiny, jeweled poker chip inside. "I didn't want photographs or anything that would give us away," he told her, carefully watching her face for a reaction.

"It's perfect," she told him, gently running her fingertip over it.

"Here, let me put it on you." Paul held his cigarette between his lips as he took the piece of jewelry, stepped behind her, and latched it at the back of her neck. His hands rested on her shoulders momentarily before sliding over her soft skin to her chest.

One of her arms snaked up behind her to touch his upper arm. "Why, I think you're just marking your territory, Mr. Preston."

He lifted a hand, removed the cigarette from his mouth, and exhaled before walking around to face her again. Holding his cigarette carefully between two fingers, he bent and placed a hand on each of her knees so he would be at eye level. "Maybe I am, Mrs. Fairfield."

Her smile faded at the mention of her married name.

"Do you have a problem with that?"

She maintained his eye contact as a hand darted up to feel the locket hanging on her chest. "You know the summer will be ending soon," she changed the subject. He didn't respond. "We'll be going back to the city," she continued to run her fingertips nervously over the tiny locket, "and I may never see you again."

He smiled, too confident to be pulled in by what she was saying. "So maybe it's good I marked my territory now."

She smiled, and her fingertips left the locket to bat him in the upper arm. "You're awful."

He smirked before leaning forward to give her a slow, yearning kiss.

Her fingertips entangled themselves in his thick, dark hair as she lost herself in the moment until he pulled back to look at her.

"So what's going to happen?" she asked.

He kissed her cheek. "Well, we could keep going on like this, and I'll see you next summer," he offered.

She felt herself melting under his touch. "Like some kind of ongoing summer fling?"

He kissed her neck again. "Something like that."

She pulled the cigarette nub from his fingers. "And the other option?" she asked before taking the final draw on the nub and setting it in the ashtray.

His lips moved up to her ear. "I'm not offering other options," his deep, steady voice whispered.

Phyllis felt the smoke become entrapped in her lungs. Using her free arm, she pushed him back. "Is that all I am to you? Some cheap, summer fling?" The smoke escaped with her words. "See you next summer, and that's it?"

Not moving his hands from her knees he was leaning on, he looked her in the eye. "Why, you're a married woman, Mrs. Fairfield. That's all we're capable of."

Phyllis pushed him harder, causing him to step back and stand. She searched his eyes, wondering if he could be serious. "So you were just using me?"

Paul leaned against the table, picked up the pack of cigarettes, and calmly tapped the end of it on the tabletop. "What did you think would happen, Mrs. Fairfield?" She blinked at him as tears began to pool in her eyes. His eyes looked coldly at hers. "After all, you can't expect much from 'just a waiter.'"

She stood up and stormed past him to the door, turning when she reached the knob. "I hate you, you know."

He calmly kept his back to her, tapping the cigarette package on the table. "Hate is a strong word for someone who doesn't even believe in love."

"Ugh!" she let out the exasperated sound before she threw the door open. "You're impossible!" She stormed out, slamming the door behind her.

Paul stood calmly tapping the cigarettes as minutes ticked by before she threw the door open again.

"I really hate this," she said in a softer voice, slamming the door closed behind her.

Paul turned just in time for her to throw herself into his arms. Her lips met his as her hands wound around his neck and became intertwined with his hair. "Don't do this to me," she whimpered into his ear when he kissed her neck. "Please don't."

CHAPTER 22

"Good Lord, you look like you just got back from Afghanistan," Judy commented when Kylie walked into her shop, slipping Cupcake into the office.

"Be nice to me, Aunt Judy, there's still a chance I could have a concussion."

She chuckled to herself. "Too late to go with that story. Chief Lange already called me and filled me in."

Kylie turned back to her aunt. "He called you?"

Her aunt was still smiling. "Well, it's procedure to inform the next of kin."

Kylie shook her head. "I can't believe he's going around telling people what happened."

"Just the next of kin," Aunt Judy corrected, holding up an index finger. "Although I've got to say, the falling through the floor was a gem of a story."

"Hey, it made sense that there would be something to step on down there."

"Yeah," Judy drew out the word as she said it, indicating her lack of belief. "But, if you didn't feel anything, it sure made sense to go ahead and jump right in."

Kylie's cheeks brightened a shade of pink as she tightened her lips into a line and turned her back to her aunt. "Did you clear out the till for the day?" she asked, changing the subject as she made her way to the front counter.

"Not yet, dear. I'm recovering from hip surgery, so I'm moving a little slower."

Kylie popped open the cash drawer to do a count.

"Although I have less bandages than you to show for it," her aunt mumbled under her breath.

"I heard that," Kylie responded without turning.

Judy chuckled to herself. "After you drop that money off at the bank, it would be nice if you stopped in to see Madeline. She's been asking about Cupcake."

"Aunt Judy, I have a shop to run and a house to renovate."

"Ten minutes. It's on your way home."

Kylie thought a minute as she tapped the bank bag on the countertop. "I would like to tell her we found the tunnel," she mused to herself.

"The perfect conversation starter," Judy commented dryly.

"I'll tell Sam you said hi," Kylie got the dig in.

"Don't you dare!"

Cupcake's toenails clicked on the shiny tile floor of Harbor Bluffs as she pulled Kylie along to Madeline's room.

Madeline wasn't in her chair as before but instead lay in bed. Kylie knocked softly on the door frame before Cupcake pulled the leash out of her hand, darted across the room, and jumped onto the bed.

Startled, the centenarian drew in a sharp breath before

quickly recognizing her friend. "Well, hello there, little girl," she said as she stroked Cupcake's head. "Did you miss me?"

Cupcake walked in several circles before snuggling herself in next to Madeline, who giggled in delight.

"Hi, Madeline," Kylie said as she stepped across the room to the bedside chair. "Cupcake and I thought we'd stop by and see how you're doing."

Madeline dropped her head heavily against the pillow. "Tired, darling. I'm so tired." She lifted her head slightly again to look at Kylie. "But you look like you've been hit by a bus."

Kylie glanced down at her arm bandages. "Just some renovation injuries," she dismissed easily.

Madeline dropped her head back again as one hand continued to stroke Cupcake, who rolled onto her back to turn it into a tummy rub.

"I have some news," Kylie offered, trying to brighten the mood in the room. "I found the tunnel you told us about."

Madeline turned her head on the pillow. "The tunnel?"

"Yes. The tunnel going from the garage to the room with the incinerator."

Madeline smiled softly as she stared up at the ceiling. "That used to be our favorite."

"Favorite?"

She turned her head to look at the young blonde seated next to her with short hair. "The incinerator room is where the kitchen used to be."

"In the basement?"

Madeline smiled and nodded. "The basement is where everything happened in that place." Her eyes looked into the distance as she continued. "Willy and I spent countless evenings lying on our elbows and peering through the screen into the kitchen. People in the kitchen knew everything that happened in that place." She focused on Kylie. "I supposed it was our form of television." She let out a soft chuckle. "It was great entertainment."

"Madeline, when you say that was your favorite tunnel, that kind of suggests there were other tunnels."

The old woman chuckled another soft chuckle. "Yes, there was another tunnel. A bigger one."

Kylie's eyes widened. "Bigger? How did you access it?"

Madeline thought a moment before answering. "I don't know."

Kylie's heart sank.

"Willy said it didn't have a screened viewing area like the one through the garage, so we weren't really interested in following it up to the club."

"But you saw it?"

Madeline smiled again at her memories. "Oh, yes. Willy and I spent a lot of time there. Those tunnels became the only place we could safely be together once my father forbade us from seeing each other."

Kylie nodded in understanding, eager to move on to her point. "So where did it come out at, Madeline?"

Madeline smiled at the bandaged blonde. "Why at the airport, dear."

Kylie looked shocked. "That far away?"

"Like the garage, it made for fast escapes and was also the perfect way to sneak anything or anyone in or out of the club."

"Wow," Kylie whispered in awe. "And you're sure it started in the basement? Because we've looked all over and can't find anything."

"Never having followed it, I'm not sure where it came out; but, as I said, the basement is where everything happened in that place."

Kylie nodded in understanding, reaching her hand up to fidget with the chain around her neck as her mind wandered. "Are there any more tunnels?"

Madeline shrugged. "I don't know. Willy used to say there were so many secrets in that place that it reminded him of a Hollywood movie."

Kylie nodded again before standing. "Well, Cupcake and I should let you rest." She reached for the puppy who let out a loud, yawning groan.

"You come back and see me again, Cupcake," Madeline told the puppy.

"Oh, she will," Kylie assured, bending to lift the dog off of the bed. "She really likes you."

Madeline kept a hand on the puppy as Kylie lifted her to her chest, and the old woman's expression changed. "What a beautiful locket you have," she commented with squinted eyes trying to get a better look.

Kylie's hand moved self-consciously to the piece of jewelry she had started wearing since she found it. "Oh, thank you." She straightened with Cupcake under one arm. "Thanks for the visit," she concluded as she turned and stepped towards the door.

Madeline's gaze followed her. "I used to have one just like that," she said softly, causing Kylie to freeze her stride in the door frame. "I used to," she repeated more softly.

Kylie turned back and stepped forward, wrapping both arms around Cupcake. "What happened to it?"

Madeline placed a hand under her head as she remembered. "I lost it when there was a fire."

Kylie stepped forward again, intrigued. "Lost it where?"

She shook her head slowly. "I'm not sure." Madeline got that far away look in her eyes again. "Willy and I were watching people in the kitchen one night." She took a slow breath. "One of the men spilled hot grease near the gas stove, and it somehow caught fire. It was just a few feet from our faces when it ignited." She swallowed hard. "We're lucky we didn't get serious burns."

Kylie sat down in the chair next to the bed again, this time keeping Cupcake on her lap.

"By the time we scooted back through the low part of the tunnel to where we could stand, it had filled with smoke." She looked at the young girl and snapped her fingers. "Just like that."

Kylie nodded, enthralled by the story.

"There was mass hysteria in the club as it, too, filled with smoke and people tried to get out. There were screams, and a panic filled the air like I've never known before."

"So did you and Willy climb out?"

"We did, but it wasn't easy. We couldn't see a thing, and it was difficult to breathe. We felt our way along the edge of the tunnel until we found the stairs." She focused in on Kylie. "I was so afraid. I thought that might be it for us, and no one would ever find us."

"But Willy got you out?"

She smiled for the first time since the story started. "Yes. Willy never let go of my hand. Even when I panicked, he kept talking to me, encouraging me to keep going. I was terrified." A tear escaped an eye and ran down her cheek. "We never went down that tunnel again."

Moments passed as Kylie took in the story.

"And what happened to your locket?"

The woman focused in on Kylie's locket again. "After we got out, there was an exodus of panicked people leaving the club. I remember people screaming as Willy and I made our way to our bikes. It wasn't until the next day that I noticed my locket was missing."

Balancing Cupcake on her lap, Kylie undid the locket and handed it to Madeline. "Look inside. I think this might be yours."

Madeline held out a gnarled hand, and Kylie dropped the piece of jewelry into it. Madeline opened the locket and peered at the tiny photographs inside. A silent tear ran down her cheek. "That's my Willy," she whispered. "Just like I remember him, that's my Willy."

CHAPTER 23

"So are you saying you need me to rescue you again?" Chief Lange teased over the phone.

Kylie rolled her eyes. "No. I just thought it might be a good idea to have another person along in case," she thought for the right word, not wanting to give him any more satisfaction, "something happens."

"Like an accident?"

"No," she defended, her mind still searching for a more reasonable excuse. "I might need you to," she thought of a suitable replacement for "rescue me," and came up with, "lift something."

She could tell he was smiling when he responded. "Okay, I'll be over in an hour. Do you want me to wear my hunky outfit?"

Kylie blushed. "Only if you're on duty," came her nonchalant response.

The sky was bright blue with white seagulls screeching in it as Kylie, Cupcake, and Chief Lange made their way through Kylie's heavily wooded backyard to the crumbling three-foot-high stacked stone wall that surrounded what was once a popular club.

"Cupcake, come," Kylie commanded the puppy who had been running around exploring. "Time to put on your leash."

Chief Lange stepped easily over a crumbling low part of the wall and turned back. "Hand me Cupcake."

Kylie did so and followed him over the wall. As the three walked down the sloping hillside to M-119, what was once named 131, it occurred to Kylie to reach for the chief's hand, but she held back. He wore jeans with his hands casually tucked into the front pockets. As Kylie lingered a step behind with Cupcake's leash before crossing the road, she noted that Aunt Judy was right, he did look good both coming and going.

"Did Madeline tell you if the tunnel comes out in a hangar similar to the garage tunnel?" the chief asked.

"Huh?" Kylie snapped out of her daydream. "Uh, no. She just said it was somewhere at the airport."

She trotted to keep up with his swift stride across the busy roadway.

"I guess we should start by looking for a hangar that backs up to the hillside then," he decided.

"This seems like a pretty open area," Kylie commented as they walked through the tall grass and down the steep hillside. "Seems like it would be difficult to hide much of anything around here."

The chief stood at the base of the hill, scanning the scrubby bushes and saplings that occupied the overgrown area. "The bad news is that none of the hangars back up to the hillside."

"So it doesn't come out in a hangar?"

His eyes remained on the buildings thoughtfully. "Unless it comes up through the bottom of one." He looked back to where the house was, and she saw him lining it up with the hillside in his mind. He nodded ahead. "This lines up with the house over here. If the tunnel is a straight shot, it may come out over here." He started to move forward.

"This is nearly a quarter mile away," Kylie observed. "The other tunnel wasn't nearly that long." She took a few quick steps to catch up with him.

"It seems like a long shot, but each tunnel had a similar purpose, so it's not unlikely it would go to the airport."

Kylie and Cupcake followed the chief along the hillside densely populated by bushes and saplings.

"Stick close to where the hillside stops," he instructed. "It's the most likely spot for an outlet. And, like the entrance to the other tunnel, it may only be three feet high, so keep your eyes low."

Kylie walked along silently, her jeans catching on prickly branches and undergrowth. "I think we're right across the road from the house now," she observed their location.

"Yep," the chief agreed as he started pulling back saplings on the hillside.

Kylie stepped past him and stopped as she spotted black

metal grating ahead. "There," she whispered as she lifted a hand to point.

The chief stopping his enthusiastic batting of bushes to look up, his body straightening to take in the arched opening with thick, black grating over it.

The two looked at each other with wide eyes before moving slowly towards the tunnel outlet.

Perfectly concealed by undergrowth and slightly set into the hillside, Kylie understood why the tunnel had gone undiscovered. If you weren't readily looking for it, you would never notice it.

Silently, the two let Cupcake lead them the fifteen feet ahead to the large piece of thick, black iron grating that covered the opening. Kylie peered inside before turning to the chief. "Give me your flashlight."

He plucked the flashlight off of his waistband and handed it to her.

Shining the light inside, she moved it from top to bottom.

"It looks just like the other tunnel. Even the cobblestone lining is the same."

The chief examined the perimeter of the grate before wrapping thick fingers around it to rattle it.

"It's locked," Kylie said, disappointment heavy in her voice.

The chief moved to the left and ran his fingertips along the edge where it met the stone wall. "There has to be some sort of a latch," he mumbled. Finding none, he reached his hand inside the grate. Kylie heard a small popping sound. "Got it!" he exclaimed.

Kylie stepped back as the chief pulled open the heavy, hinged grate.

"Sure wish I brought a couple of hard hats," he mumbled, peering into the tunnel. He glanced at his fellow explorer. "Especially for you."

"Shut up," Kylie admonished, stepping bravely into the opening with the flashlight.

He grabbed her arm and pulled her back. "In all seriousness, why don't you let me go first."

Kylie stomped her foot. "The last time you went first, this happened," she answered, pointing an index finger to the butterfly bandage on her head.

He suppressed a smile. "Okay, lead the way."

Kylie kept Cupcake's leash short as the three entered the tunnel that exactly resembled the previous one they had discovered.

"I can't believe how long this is," Kylie muttered as she aimed the flashlight at the top and then the bottom of the tunnel.

"Must be a quarter mile," the chief agreed.

There was a loud rumble ahead, and bits of dirt dropped from the ceiling.

The chief grabbed her arm again. "I really think we should go back and get hard hats."

"We're already halfway through," Kylie exaggerated. "We'll

be okay if we made it this far."

"I don't think fifty yards is half way, but you're the boss," he responded, reluctantly releasing her arm.

There were only a few more steps taken before Kylie announced, "Dead end."

The chief took the flashlight from Kylie's hand where it was aimed at a wall of dirt and pointed it to the top of the tunnel. "Looks like it caved in."

Another loud rumble came from above, and more bits of dirt fell onto the explorers.

"Trucks," he thought aloud.

"Hmm," Kylie mused as they both watched the ceiling expectantly.

"The heavy vibrations must have caused this portion to eventually cave in." His flashlight moved slowly down the dirt wall in front of them.

"Well, how will we ever find the – " Kylie's comment was interrupted by her ear-piercing scream as the chief's light came to rest on what was left of a human hand. On one finger was a large gem that reflected back the light. The scream echoed through the tunnel, and larger amounts of dirt followed by cobblestones began to fall as the chief grabbed Kylie's arm again.

CHAPTER 24

Paul Preston sat at the closed basement bar, sipping an early evening drink before the crowds arrived. Willy silently slipped onto the stool next to him.

Paul could hear the clanking and quiet mumbles of the prep cooks from the kitchen behind them. He didn't look at Willy to acknowledge him. "So what did you find out?"

Mirroring his mentor, Willy placed his elbows on the bar and gazed ahead, watching the man in the large mirror that was set into the ornately-carved wooden bar. "Mr. Fairfield goes into town most every day."

"For how long?"

"Most of the day."

"And Mrs. Fairfield?"

"She mostly stays at the house."

Paul nodded and took a sip of his drink. "What's Mr.

Fairfield do all day in a town this small?"

Willy hesitated to answer, worrying that it would not be well received. "He spends most of his time at Allie Walker's house."

Paul turned his head to the boy, unusually surprised.

Willy blushed. "Sometimes they go out to shops or walk down to the boats, but mostly they stay at her house."

Paul's voice registered his disbelief. "Allie Walker, as in our cigarette girl?"

Willy nodded.

"What is she? Eighteen years old?"

Willy nodded again.

Paul tightened his lips and looked back to his drink. "And Mrs. Fairfield, what does she do when her husband's away?"

Willy shrugged. "I only followed them around for a couple of days, but mostly she just sits on the front porch, staring out at the bay."

Paul nodded solemnly.

"She looks so sad," Willy observed.

Paul slowly closed and then opened his eyes before reaching into his pocket. "You did a good job, kid."

"Thanks, Mr. Preston," Willy said as he accepted the bills. He lingered for a moment, unsure how to say what he wanted to say.

Paul turned his gaze back to the boy. "You got something else?"

Willy looked at his feet as he scuffed a foot on the carpet. "About that job in Detroit at the end of the summer, Mr. Preston."

Paul nodded solemnly. "I've made the arrangements."

Willy smiled broadly. "Thank you, sir. Thank you so much!" He started to step away and then turned back, remembering something. He pulled a small box out of his pocket and set it on the bar. "Here's your collateral, sir."

Hours later, after the dinner crowd had moved downstairs, Paul stood silently across the room from the Roulette table watching Henry Fairfield. He had a feeling that the man was slowly gambling away his wife's fortune, though Phyllis had never mentioned anything about her money.

He stood observing Henry Fairfield shamelessly flirt with his cigarette girl. She would playfully tip his fedora, and his hand would casually graze her bottom. All went unnoticed in the crowded room except to the astute observer. He felt his jaw tighten as he watched.

"Miss Walker is it?" he asked when she passed by him with her cigarette tray hooked behind her neck.

"Yes, Mr. Preston?" she asked.

Paul put a strong hand on her shoulder and leaned in to her. "I'd like to see you upstairs."

Concern washed over her face. "Did I do something wrong?"

"No, not at all," he lied. "Let's just step upstairs for a minute."

Allie turned and headed towards the stairs with Paul following at a distance. His eyes stayed on Henry Fairfield. As he and Allie crossed the room, he saw Henry glance up from the Roulette wheel long enough to make eye contact with Allie. The smile disappeared from his face when he saw Allie's expression.

Paul smirked to himself. That son-of-a-bitch was about to have a lot more time available to spend with his wife.

"Mr. Preston, I didn't do anything. I swear," Allie pled as soon as she reached the top of the stairs.

"I know you haven't," Paul assured her. "To the contrary, we like the work you've been doing."

Now the young woman's concern turned to surprise. "You do?"

Paul pulled out a chair from one of the tables in the empty dining room, and Allie sat down, Paul sitting across from her. Allie fiddled with her short, blonde waves, pushing them nervously behind an ear."

"Sure. We've been watching you, and Mr. Gerhart and I think you have a lot of potential."

"Potential for what?" she wondered aloud.

"Now, don't underestimate the importance of your job, young lady," Paul explained. "You make up an important part of the sales at this club."

"Oh."

Paul could tell she was skeptical. "See, now, the thing is, we have a similar position available in Mr. Gerhart's Virginia Beach club, and we need someone to fill it."

"Virginia?"

"Yep. We had a girl quit last week, and we need to get it filled as soon as possible."

"As soon as possible?" the girl echoed.

Paul looked seriously at her. "I'm willing to pay your travel expenses if you can leave tomorrow and help us out with this."

"Tomorrow?"

Paul could tell she was stunned at the sudden suggestion. "Yes. There's a train leaving tomorrow afternoon, and I'd like to get you on it."

"Mr. Preston, I really appreciate your offer, Allie began to decline, "but I can't possibly leave – "

"Did I mention you'd be making double what you'd be making here?"

Her face froze. "Double?"

He turned his palms up. "It only makes sense since you have so much experience working here." He could tell she was hesitating. "Miss Walker, this is a great opportunity. The summer is almost over here, everyone will be leaving, and you'll be without employment until next summer," he watched her carefully, "if we bring you back."

Her eyes quickly focused in on his, now comprehending his intent. She blushed. "Well, yes, I believe I could have my things ready by tomorrow afternoon." She looked down at her hands and fumbled them as she spoke.

Paul leaned back in his chair, satisfied. "Good girl. I knew we could count on you."

Allie looked up at him. "Is that all?"

Paul nodded, and the young woman rose and started to walk away.

"Oh, Allie," he called after her. She turned to look back, one hand on the doorframe. "Don't tell anyone about this, okay?"

Her eyes were sad as she comprehended what he meant, and she nodded her head.

Paul nodded, feeling assured she wouldn't tell Henry Fairfield anything. "Very well. Why don't you head out and start packing."

Allie nodded to him again with those sad eyes, and Paul felt satisfied as he watched her walk away.

"Maybe, in Virginia, you'll be more selective about the company you keep, Miss Walker," he said smugly to himself.

CHAPTER 25

Two police cars and two sheriff's vehicles lined the edge of the airport as Kylie stood at one of the open vehicle doors, a blanket wrapped around both her and Cupcake. The chief stood some distance away speaking with the officers.

"It's going to be okay, Cuppie," Kylie comforted the puppy in her arms before giving her a soft kiss on the head. Kylie brushed some dirt from her eyelashes before squinting to see the chief through the dusk that was setting in. "Why does he get to hear all of the good information, and we don't?" she asked the puppy.

After a few seconds, the chief glanced Kylie watching him and stepped away from the group.

"Are you two okay?" he asked, brushing some dirt from her cheek.

Kylie hugged Cupcake closer. "Shaken up but okay."

He nodded. "We were lucky. If the majority of the tunnel that ran under the road had not already been caved in, things might have turned out differently."

Kylie nodded solemnly and pulled the plaid blanket closer as she remembered the gruesome sight she had seen as stones and piles of dirt fell on them.

"I told you we should have worn hard hats."

"Next time," she agreed before adding, "but try not to gloat."

He let out a soft chuckle.

"So is there some kind of law enforcement code of confidentiality, or can you tell me if they know whose hand it was?" Kylie asked, gripping her puppy close to her for comfort.

"No," he answered, shaking his head before pulling the blanket tighter around her.

"'No,' there's no code or, 'no,' they don't know who the hand belonged to?"

"No, they don't know who it belongs to."

"Are they going to dig her up?" Kylie asked, assuming from the jeweled ring that it was the body of a woman.

"Eventually. They'll need to bring in some engineers first to reinforce the tunnel before they can excavate. It could be a while." He brushed loose dirt from her hair.

"It's on you too, you know," she pointed out.

"I'm sure it is." He watched her with his confident, calm smile he always seemed to have around her. "You might want to make a mental note that screaming in a hundred-year-old tunnel is never a good idea."

She rolled her eyes before shivering. "To think I had a person buried under my house all this time."

"Well, it's not really under your house."

"But it connects to my house."

"We'll find out." He looked amused.

She shivered again. "It's like a grave opening right into the place. Right below my bedroom. I'm surprised the smell of rotting flesh didn't keep me awake at night," she started to carry on.

Now he smiled, unable to hold back his look of amusement. "Yeah, yeah," he acknowledged, reaching one strong arm around her and Cupcake and then the other, squeezing them in close. "I think that flesh rotted a long time ago."

Kylie didn't fight the affection and turned her head to rest on his strong chest. "Maybe Madeline will know who it is."

"Maybe." She felt him lay his head on her dirt-covered hair.

She momentarily cheered and lifted her head to look at him. "You know, there is one good thing about this."

"What?"

She smiled up at him. "You didn't have to rescue me today."

CHAPTER 25

"I've got something for you, Sam," Kylie announced to Sam Shepard as she spotted him in the halls of Harbor Bluffs.

The retired librarian in a wheelchair perked up. "Ya don't say."

"Yup," Kylie informed as she held out the gray cardboard box with the cellophane window in it. "Aunt Judy asked me to deliver it to you," she lied.

Cupcake jumped against the man's knees in an effort to see what was in the box.

"Is that your dog?"

Kylie blushed. "Yes. Sorry, she's a little excitable." She reached down and scooped up the puppy.

Refocusing on the box, a slow smile spread across his face. "You say Judy sent this?"

"Yup," Kylie lied again.

"Ooh, I knew it," he glowed as he fumbled with the top of the box. "It's a cupcake."

"Yup." She leaned over and helped him fold back the lid. "It's called Love Spell."

"Love Spell? What kind of name is that for a cupcake?"

"I don't know," Kylie played dumb, "but you should try it."

Sam peeled back part of the cupcake wrapper. "Sure is the biggest cupcake I've ever seen."

"It's fifty-percent frosting," Kylie said proudly.

"The best part."

"I couldn't agree more," Kylie glowed as he took a bite, getting frosting all around his mouth. "I've always said a cupcake is just a vehicle for frosting."

He smiled and took another bite.

"When do you get out, Sam?"

"In just a few days." He took a third bite, thoroughly

enjoying the dessert.

"You should stop by the shop sometime and thank Judy," she suggested with a sly smile on her face as she stepped away.

"Ooh, I'll do that, I'll do that," he agreed enthusiastically. He held up an index finger to her. "You know, I just knew she was sweet on me."

Kylie threw him a smile that concealed her secret. "Nothing gets past you, Sam."

Leaving Sam to enjoy his cupcake, Kylie set Cupcake down and proceeded down the hallway of Harbor Bluffs. Anxious to see her friend, Cupcake led the way, pulling Kylie along behind her.

"What happened?" Kylie asked, dumbfounded when she rounded the corner to find an empty bed. "Where's Madeline?"

Two nurses stood whispering near a cardboard box. "She passed away last night," one of them said, acknowledging her question.

Kylie felt a wave of sadness rush over her. "Did she have

any family or friends around?"

The nurse shook her head. "Not really. Once you pass ninety years old, it's likely you've outlived all of your friends."

Kylie nodded. "Do you have an address for her daughter?"

The nurse shook her head again. "She has no next of kin listed. As a matter of fact, we were just discussing what to do with her box of things."

Kylie's eyes moved to the box. "May I?"

One of the nurses shrugged and stepped back.

Kylie stepped forward, holding Cupcake's leash with one hand and moving around the contents of the box with the other. She fished out the locket Kylie had just given her back that had been so precious to her. Turning to the nurses, she said, "She should be buried in this. It was very important to her."

One of the nurses held out a hand, and Kylie dropped the locket into it. "I'll take care of it," the woman assured.

Kylie continued to sift through the box of framed old photos, a couple of puzzles, medications, and a couple of small, stuffed animals. At the bottom she found an old scrapbook and pulled it out. Turning a few pages, she saw photos of Madeline when she was a young girl all the way up to the card she'd received from the President. Gesturing to the nurses, she asked, "Mind if I keep this?"

One shrugged and scooped up the box. "Fine with me. The rest will just go in the garbage."

"I can't believe she's gone," Kylie whispered more to herself than the remaining nurse.

Hours later, Kylie sat at her Aunt Judy's kitchen table, looking through the scrapbook full of memories.

"I can't believe she could fit her whole life into one scrapbook," Judy commented, using her reading glasses to examine some of the old black-and-white photographs.

"It's kind of sad," Kylie said. She turned to a page that contained one of the photos of Willy. "This was her soul mate,

Willy. They were madly in love, but her father wouldn't let them be together."

Judy leaned in and looked at the photo closer as Kylie continued on. "Now, who is he with in this photo?" She flipped it over and read it aloud. "Willy and Mr. Preston." Kylie looked back at the photo. "Hmm, he's a good-looking guy."

Judy was still looking at the first photograph and adjusted her glasses again as she leaned in closer. "Just a minute." Without another word, Judy got up and rolled her walker into the living room.

"Willy and Maddie," Kylie mused to herself, flipping back to the front of another photo to view the love-struck teenagers. She ran her fingertips over the photograph. "She was so beautiful," she whispered.

Kylie was about to turn the page when she heard some banging and thuds and then a triumphant, "Here it is!"

Rolling back in, Judy set an old photograph on the table

before she sat down.

Kylie picked it up and examined it. "Aunt Judy, why do you have a picture of Willy?"

Judy smiled at her niece. "Because it's your Great Grandpa Bill."

CHAPTER 26

"If I were a secret tunnel, I would be behind this plaster," Kylie told Cupcake as she pried ancient plaster from the south wall of her basement, revealing the cement block walls behind it.

Her phone dinged its signal that a text message had come on. Dropping her crowbar, she pulled her phone from her back pocket.

"You'd better not be looking for a tunnel," she read aloud.

She looked down at the little pit mix puppy sitting near her feet. "If the chief thinks I'm waiting weeks for bodies to be exhumed so we can find out where that tunnel comes out, he's wrong."

She looked back to her phone. "Don't worry," she texted back. She looked down at the puppy and said, "That way I'm not lying."

She heard a ding behind her and spun around to see the chief standing at the base of the stairs reading her text. "Don't worry, huh?" he asked, looking up from his phone.

Cupcake ran to yip at the intruder.

"Nice work, watchdog," Kylie commented dryly before looking up to the chief. "Don't you knock?"

"I did. No answer, so I texted."

"So you thought you'd just break in?"

"The front door was wide open."

Kylie tightened her lips together, remembering it was a beautiful day, and she had left it open to air the place out a bit. "Well, what are you doing here anyway?"

He crossed his arms and leaned against the wall at the base of the stairs. "I was pretty sure you wouldn't take my advice." He held two stacked hard hats up with one hand and gestured towards the wall with his head. "Looks to me like you're not waiting for the tunnel to be reinforced and cleared."

Her shoulders slumped guiltily forward. "I mean aren't you

curious?" She turned and gestured to the wall. "Like, it has to be around here somewhere."

He watched her calmly, maintaining his stance. "The thing about secret passages is that they wouldn't want to tear apart walls every time they used them."

Kylie looked back at her demo work and thought a moment. "Well, maybe someone put paneling or plaster over it later on without knowing."

He shrugged. "Maybe."

She lifted the crowbar and spun it like a heavy baton as her eyes twinkled at the walls. "So you think I don't need this?"

"Probably not."

"What would you suggest?"

Holding his spot, he casually suggested, "I'd look for a latch or switch."

Kylie looked frustrated. "I've been over these walls fifty

times, and even you went over them." She turned to look at the torn-up wall before her. "I don't see anything."

"Want some help?"

Kylie shrugged, and the chief stepped off of the last step. Hands on the cement, the two went over the south wall inch by inch.

"It's not here," Kylie said, dropping her hands in frustration. "Maybe the tunnel starts off of another wall."

The chief gazed at the southeast corner of the building. "It's possible," he conceded.

"I mean the one off of the kitchen was on the north wall but came out to the east," Kylie pointed out." He didn't respond, and she followed his gaze. "You think it's in one of the bathrooms?"

"It's the only part of the wall we haven't covered."

"It's just old wallpaper falling off the walls in there. Nowhere to put a latch."

Ignoring her, the chief strode across the damp cement floor to the first bathroom and put his hand on the doorknob. "You check the ladies room, I'll take this one," he smirked at her.

"Okaaaay," Kylie conceded. "But I've already looked in here."

"Cover it inch by inch," he instructed before disappearing into the men's room with blue shredded wallpaper hanging from its walls.

"Come on, Cuppie, you're a girl," Kylie told the puppy who followed her into the room.

Switching on the overhead light, Kylie reached up and placed her palms against the wall, slowly moving them over the brittle old wallpaper. She tapped her hand occasionally to see if there was anything behind it.

"Find anything yet?" she heard the chief yell from next door.

"Nope. You?"

"Nope."

"Keep looking."

As her hands reached chest level, she tapped a spot, and the wallpaper gave. Tapping again, she saw it indent into an opening, popping back out when she removed the pressure from her hand. She looked down at Cupcake with wide eyes before slipping her hand behind the wallpaper to feel a handle. Giving it a light tug, the wall easily moved towards her.

"Watch out, Cupcake," she whispered to the puppy who understood enough to scoot behind her owner.

Keeping her hand on the handle, she stepped back and pulled the wall of cement blocks open with surprising ease.

"Chief!" she screamed in delight. "Chief, I found it!"

Within seconds, Chief Lange was at the door, the two hard hats under one arm.

"Wow, a door of cement blocks," he commented with admiration in his voice as he ran his hand down the iron frame surrounding it.

Kylie's heart was thumping as she stepped into the hidden room and saw the shelves of dust-covered poker chips lining the wall. "Wow," she whispered, running her fingers over a row of chips before pulling one out to inspect it. "It's been frozen in time."

The chief stepped in, slipping his hands casually into his front pockets as he looked up at the ceiling and then lowered his eyes to rest on the Roulette wheel in the corner. "This must be where they hid stuff during raids."

Kylie turned to the wall behind her and saw a few bottles of liquor left on them, a heavy layer of dust covering them as well. She lifted one of them and blew on the label. "Gin," she said wiggling it at her fellow explorer. "Flavored with juniper berries."

He smiled at her. "We'll have to try it later."

She set the bottle back on the shelf, stepped to the doorway, and looked about the room. "As cool as this is, we still haven't found the tunnel entrance."

He nodded, his hands still hanging in his pockets as he

looked about the room. "There's always a chance it could start outside."

Kylie nodded. "Did you finish looking in the men's room? Is there a door like this in there?"

"Nope. Most of the wallpaper has fallen off of the wall in there, so I would have spotted something like this easily," he indicated to the doorframe.

Kylie leaned on the rusty iron doorframe and stared at the wall of shelves before her. Cupcake positioned herself next to Kylie's feet and mirrored her owner.

Chief Lange started lightly stomping the cement floor along the base of the shelves.

"What are you doing?"

Without looking up from his stomping, he said, "The entrance in the garage is through a trap door. I thought there might be one here."

"But that's a wooden floor in a cabinet. This is cement,"

Kylie pointed out.

He paused to tilt his head towards the door. "So is that."

Kylie nodded and let him finish as she looked about the room. "Do you see how all of the shelves on this wall have chips and cards on them except for these two in the center and this one over here?" she pointed to the third shelf on the left.

The chief looked where she was pointing. "You think it's under shelves like in the garage?" He shook his head. "I checked the floor underneath there, it's not hollow."

Kylie shook her head. "I think it's similar but – " She stepped forward and lifted out the two empty shelves, placing them on the empty one.

The chief stepped into the space and stomped his foot on the floor. "Nothing."

Kylie shook her head. "Don't you see how this is the center of the shelves? When you remove the bottom two, it makes an opening large enough for an adult to easily duck under. She stepped forward and placed her palms on the bead board shelf backing. Her eyes scanned the perimeter. "It seems like I should just be able to – " She leaned in, and the back of the shelving unit easily turned into a door that swung open with a painful squeak from rusted hinges. Kylie drew in a breath.

"Got it," the chief announced in a hushed tone.

Cupcake scampered by Kylie's feet towards the tunnel.

"Oh, no, you don't," Kylie said, scooping the puppy into her arms. "You're sticking with me." The puppy licked Kylie's cheek happily.

"Your hat, madam," the chief said, holding out a hard hat.

"Man, you think of everything," she thanked him before stepping into the tunnel.

"Wait," he warned, grabbing her arm and holding her back.

"What?"

"Remember, no matter what, no screaming in the tunnel."

CHAPTER 27

Judy was sitting on a stool behind the front display case in Kylie Kakes when the front door opened.

"Hello?" Judy called from her stool, leaning to see who had opened it.

"I'm working on it," came a man's voice before Judy saw Sam Shepard push his walker through the doorway. "This isn't the most handicap-accessible place," Sam announced as he worked his way into the shop taking baby steps.

Judy's face fell. "Well, I get in and out just fine with my walker."

Sam's face lit up when he rounded the corner and saw Judy. "Hey, there gorgeous."

"Sam," she acknowledged him in a cool tone.

He wheeled his walker to the front display case and leaned an elbow on it. "How's my buttercup?"

"Fine, Sam." She wriggled uncomfortably. "You're looking for cupcakes?"

"Just you, Cupcake," he joked.

Judy squinted at him, not sure what had brought about the change in confidence level.

"Just wanted to come in and thank you for the cupcake you sent to me while I was recuperating."

"Cupcake?"

"It surely made my day," he beamed at her with confidence and happiness.

"Sam, I didn't – "

"Sure, you did. Kylie brought it by," he looked at a photo on the wall of Judy and Kylie together, "that sweet girl."

"Oh, she did, huh?" Judy felt her blood begin to boil.

"Yep." He leaned in to her conspiratorially, "I always thought you had your eye on me."

"Sam, I don't – "

"Which tells me it's fate because I've had my eye on you since the first time I saw you in 1974."

Judy's head moved back as if she'd seen a snake. "1974?"

"Fourth of July parade."

Judy's mind fought to remember that far back.

"You were walking with the Girl Scouts, and I leaned over and told my buddy, 'That gal can sell me cookies any day.'"

Judy blushed, both embarrassed and surprised by this sudden attention Sam was showing. "No good deed goes unpunished," she mumbled to herself as she tugged her bright yellow top down and noticed her suitor's eyes dart to her ample breasts. "Sam, why this sudden interest?"

His eyes moved back up to hers, and he smiled adoringly at her. "Ever since Kylie delivered that cupcake to me, something just clicked." He moved his hands in the air to indicate a parting motion. "It all became so clear to me," he announced before leaning his head on his hand and resting on the display case. "I just couldn't keep my feelings inside anymore."

Judy narrowed her eyes at him suspiciously. "Just what kind of cupcake did Kylie deliver to you?"

Not breaking his gaze, he lifted his hand to make a small gesture in the air as he fought to remember. "Oh, I don't know." His eyes searched the air. "Cinnamon something." He refocused on Judy and smiled. "Never had anything like it."

She continued to glare at him. "Cinnamon, nutmeg, and juniper?"

He snapped his fingers and pointed at her. "Juniper frosting, that was it." He looked dramatic as he continued. "It kind of freaked me out at first," he lifted both of his hands and wiggled them as he uttered the word not familiar to his generation, "but it was something else."

Judy's felt heat rush to her cheeks. "Love Spell? She gave you Love Spell?"

The man rested his head on his hand as he continued to gaze at her adoringly. "I didn't need no Love Spell to know the way I felt about you, Judy."

The door jingled as it flew open, and three little boys ran to the display case, placing their sticky palms against it.

Acknowledging their presence, Sam leaned in closer to Judy. "I'll save a seat for you at Bingo tonight." He held a hand out flat as he continued, "it's on me." The tone he used made it sound as if he'd just offered to fly her Italy and pay for it.

"Thanks, Sam," Judy replied dryly.

CHAPTER 28

Kylie adjusted the large hard hat on her head. "Are they supposed to be this loose?" she asked wiggling it to demonstrate.

"Hook the straps under your chin," Chief Lange instructed.

"Oh, good grief," she complained. "We're just going into a tunnel, not Mammoth Cave."

"You never know what it will turn into," the chief stated, stepping in close to tighten her chin strap. His eyes moved up to meet hers when he finished. "There."

"Thanks," she said softly, meeting his eye contact.

Cupcake squirmed in her arms.

Chief Lange smiled at the puppy. "You could probably let her run ahead. She's a pit bull, and you carry her around like she's Toto."

"Pit mix," Kylie defended the puppy, "and letting her run ahead was how this whole mess started in the first place."

"Point taken," the Chief agreed. He pulled two flashlights off of his waistband and handed one to Kylie. "Ladies first."

"I love how you come prepared." Kylie grinned a dimpled grin at him as she ducked under the remaining shelf and into the tunnel.

Her sneakers slipped along the moist cobblestones, and her flashlight cut through the darkness revealing nothing but more darkness.

"Ooh, look, it branches off," Kylie exclaimed after a hundred yards. "Should we go this way?"

The chief shined his light down the tunnel to his right. "No. See how it narrows quickly?"

"Yeah."

"My bet is this turns into your air shaft that Cupcake fell into."

"Oh." She lifted her flashlight to aim at the ceiling. "Well, we can explore it later."

He held up a hand to shield his eyes. "Good idea. Let's go."

Another two hundred yards, and they could hear the rumble of cars ahead. "This is where the problem started on the other side," Kylie observed.

"And there's the dirt wall, which tells us we've reached the other side of the caved-in tunnel that we saw before," the chief stated, pointing his light at the wall of dirt that hid a body.

They stood in silence, looking at the hidden grave. "I wonder why they just left her there," Kylie wondered aloud.

The chief slipped his hand around hers as she continued her muse.

"I mean surely someone missed her."

He gave her hand a squeeze.

She looked up at the deteriorating ceiling of the tunnel and the bits of dirt that fell every time a car passed overhead and thought a moment. "You don't think someone could have killed her on purpose, do you?" she asked, looking to the chief at her side.

"Anything is possible."

Kylie nodded sadly before letting out a sigh. "Ready to go back?"

"Lead the way."

Kylie pivoted quickly, pushing off to step at the same time, and slipped on the moist cobblestones below her.

Instinctively, the chief reached out an arm to hold her up.

"Hey!" she protested a little too loudly as larger clumps of dirt began to fall. "I told you, no more rescuing."

"So I should just let you fall next time?" He placed his hand holding the flashlight under her other arm and hoisted her back to her feet to face him.

"Maybe," she answered defiantly.

Their eyes met and held, their faces inches apart as he propped her up. "You don't have to always push me away, you know," he said softly.

"I'm not," she whispered the lie.

"You are." He inched closer.

One of Kylie's hands were gripping his arm for support, but she didn't notice. "It's a small town," she defended in her whisper. "Things could be uncomfortable if they don't work out," she pointed out, feeling vulnerable as she realized that she was close enough to the hunky firefighter to notice the light sprinkling of freckles across his nose and upper cheeks in the dim light.

"That's true."

Inches from his face, her eyes left his to focus on his lips. Moments passed as she thought about his response before she rose onto her toes, bringing her lips to his level. She felt his grip tighten on her arms. Her eyes searched his in the dim light, looking for a possibility of rejection. He maintained eye contact but didn't give her any clues as to what he was thinking. Slowly and with the uncertainty of a fawn taking its first steps, she inched her lips closer to his before closing her eyes to softly kiss him on the lips.

When she opened her eyes and pulled back, he was smiling at her.

"Now, was that so hard?" he asked.

Kylie's demeanor changed as she began to protest, but his free hand left her arm, moved to her head, and brought her lips back to his.

CHAPTER 29

"Kylie Sue!" Aunt Judy shouted as she wheeled her walker through the front door of Kylie Kakes.

"Good morning, Aunt Judy," Kylie greeted, her good mood ringing in her voice.

"Don't good morning me," young lady, Aunt Judy stormed, pausing her walker at the front display counter. "You meddled."

"Meddled in what?" Kylie played dumb, happily frosting cupcakes.

"You gave Sam Shepard one of those ridiculous Love Spell cupcakes of yours, and now he won't leave me alone."

"And that's bad because…?" Kylie asked, still smiling down at the frosting she was swirling onto a batch of chocolate cupcakes laced with cayenne pepper.

"Because he's wheeling around town after me in his walker all googly-eyed."

"Kind of like you're wheeling around town in your walker?"

"Kylie."

"How did you like having someone to sit with at Bingo last night?" she continued as she started to hum to herself.

"It was awful. He wouldn't stop talking, and he kept trying to buy my love with Bingo cards."

Kylie's smile widened. "Did it work?"

"No!" her aunt exclaimed, her frustration bordering on anger. "And how did you know I sat next to him at Bingo?"

"A little bird might have whispered a suggestion in his ear."

Judy began to shake. "You started this, and you need to make it stop. Don't you have something to counteract the spell?"

Kylie lifted the finished tray of cupcakes and walked to where her aunt was at the front display. Sliding open the door of the case, she asked, "Oh, come on, Aunt Judy, you don't believe in spells." She slid the large tray into the display and stood up again.

"Spells are right up there with Bigfoot and secret tunnels."

"I don't but – "

"So it must be true love," Kylie finished for her.

The door jingled before her aunt could start another round of chastising, and Chief Lange stepped in.

"Good morning, Judy," he greeted cheerfully before stepping to the display case.

Leaning over it, he put a finger under Kylie's chin to lift it and kissed her softly on the lips. "Good morning, Sunshine."

Aunt Judy's jaw fell.

"Good morning," Kylie replied, all smiles.

"Oh, no, she did it to you, too," Judy declared.

"Did what?" Chief Lange broke his eye contact with Kylie and turned to her aunt.

Judy leaned onto the display to get closer and whispered conspiratorially, "She slipped you one of those Love Spell cupcakes."

The chief smiled at the upset woman. "She did?"

"Didn't she?"

The chief crossed his arms. "Actually, Judy, I've been very careful to avoid the Love Spell cupcakes."

"You were?"

He glanced at Kylie before continuing. "However, if she did slip me one, I don't think it would be the worst thing that ever happened to me."

"Oh, it is," Judy assured him. "It's horrible. People walk around with hearts and flowers in their eyes and can't keep their hands off of each other."

"You seem pretty worked up," he observed. "Did she slip you one?"

"Oh, God, no," Judy's hand flew to her throat. "I know better. She could never slip me one." She leaned in for emphasis before continuing. "She slipped one to Sam Shepard."

Chief Lange chuckled. "Ol' Sam, huh? Seems like you two would be a good match."

"No, we're not," Judy stormed. "He's a librarian."

"So?"

"All he does is talk about books," she said it like it was a dirty word, "and try to grope me." She tugged her shirt down sharply to emphasize her disposition.

The chief chuckled again. "If it bothers you so much and you believe in spells, why don't you just eat a cupcake too?"

"I don't believe in spells," she assured him.

"Then it can't hurt. If you don't feel any differently, maybe his affections are true."

Judy narrowed her eyes and pointed a finger at him. "I see where you're going with this, but it's not going to work."

"I didn't think I'd get one by you, Judy," he confirmed.

She tightened her lips together, still upset. "Yeah, well, I'll be in the office with Cupcake if you need me. At least I don't have to worry about her casting love spells."

"She'll be happy to see you, Aunt Judy," Kylie beamed back.

Judy pushed her walker past the display case and towards the back of the building.

Kylie leaned happily on the display case as she gazed at the handsome chief before her. "So what brings you in, Chief?"

He leaned back to return her gaze. "Well," his eyes glanced down at her lips and then back up before he continued, "two things."

"I hope one of them is me," she flirted.

He grinned. "Okay, three things." Unable to resist any longer, he leaned in and gave her another kiss, this one lingering. "No, four things," he added as he pulled back.

She smiled blissfully. "So what are the other two?"

He dropped his weight to his elbows on the display case. "First, I thought I'd see if you need any more help on your house projects since I have the afternoon off today."

"Hmm," she dropped to her elbows to match his height. "I get off at ten this morning, so that's definitely a possibility."

His smile twitched as he realized how much he liked it when she flirted with him.

"And what's the other thing?"

His face sobered. "They've found another body in your tunnel."

Kylie's color left her face. "Two bodies?"

His green eyes told her yes.

"Well, have they excavated all the way through? What if there are more? What if there are, like, ten?" She started to panic. "What if I've got some kind of gangster graveyard connected to my house?" Her mind wandered further. "Oh, God, what if that's where the gangsters buried their victims?" She focused on something behind the chief. "I wonder if it's too late to get my money back on the house?" Her focus changed again. "Isn't there some kind of ordinance for graveyards?" Her head dropped. "There is. I know there is. The city will sue me." She looked up again. "I'm outside the city limit. The county will sue me." Her focus changed again. "Or the state or – "

The chief's hand moved to cover one of hers and calm her. "They've dug all the way through. There's just two."

"Oh." Kylie cleared her throat and made an effort to regain her composure. "Do they know who they are – were?" she corrected herself.

He nodded. "They had identification on them."

CHAPTER 30

As soon as the secret door closed behind them, Paul pushed Phyllis against the wall of the tunnel and pressed a hand over her mouth. He saw panic in her eyes and eased his grip. "Don't move, and don't say a word until the raid is over," he whispered next to her ear.

She nodded with large eyes, and he removed his hand from her mouth, his body remaining pressed against hers, their faces inches from each other.

Phyllis listened for what seemed like an eternity as bottles clinked on the other side of the wall as the crates were stacked into what little empty space was left in the room. The wall thudded next to them as tray after tray of poker chips was quickly stacked on top of the other, the rush apparent by the clumsy thuds.

After a while, she heard the concrete door close and the voices fade followed by a barrage of gunshots flying off of the steel door and more screams. She let out a gasp as bits of dirt fell with each gunshot that sounded and then echoed through the tunnel.

"They're out of the safe room," Paul whispered, not moving away from her. "We can whisper, but I don't want to risk running out until the raid is over."

Phyllis nodded her understanding. "They got all of the liquor in the club into that tiny room?"

He shook his head, remaining close to her. "There are two more safe rooms behind the bar. Most of it was stashed in there."

She nodded again, and he watched her closely.

"Are you okay?"

She nodded again, keeping her eyes on his. His hands found hers hanging at her side and gripped them.

"Will they come in here?"

He shook his head. "This tunnel is only used for liquor imports from the airport. If they need to get away, they'll take the tunnel to the garage."

"There's another tunnel?"

He gave her a small smile. "Al built this place expecting raids and not expecting to get caught."

She nodded again, the fear quickly turning into excitement as his body remained pressed against hers.

"So we're leaving?"

Now it was his turn to nod.

"My husband will look for me."

"He won't find you."

Her eyes pled to his. "If he does, I don't think I'll survive."

He nodded grimly. "I've got you."

She released one of his hands and lifted a finger to his lips, touching them thoughtfully. "There's something I should talk to you about."

He smirked. "You're not going to tell me you believe in love, are you?"

She smiled and shook her head. "No. Of course not."

He leaned his free arm on the wall behind her. "Good, because that's one of the things I love about you."

Her focus left his lips, her fingertip dropping to his chin as her eyes moved back to meet his in surprise.

He leaned in to kiss her, and she inched her head away from his. "Paul, I really think we should talk about something before I leave with you."

His nose rubbed hers momentarily as his free hand began to gather up the skirt of her dress to lift it. His mouth came to hers, and her fingertip left his chin and slid to the side of his jaw, encouraging him.

His mouth moved to her cheek and then her ear as he whispered, "You've already left with me." He kissed her earlobe. "Tell me later. I'm going to have forever with you."

CHAPTER 31

Kylie slipped into the chair next to Chief Lange on the opposite side of the desk from the county coroner. One of the state troopers pulled up an additional chair.

"Paul Preston and Phyllis Fairfield," the coroner announced, leaning back and folding his hands across his protruding belly, his long, gray hair floating loosely around his face despite the bald spot on top.

"That's who the dead people are – were?" Kylie asked, correcting herself again, unsure how to refer to the bodies found in the tunnel that connected to her house.

"Yep," the coroner confirmed.

Kylie looked at the other people in the room with big eyes. "How do you know?"

The coroner leaned over and lifted a small, cardboard box off of the floor and set it on his desk, sliding it towards Kylie. "This is what was found on them," he shrugged, "along with the fragments left of their clothing."

Kylie leaned forward and looked into the box. On one side of it she spotted a woman's clutch with an embroidered pattern on it. There was a man's wallet, a watch, the large sapphire ring she had seen on the dead hand, and a thin chain that she spotted peeking out from under everything else.

"Do I get to keep this?" she asked.

The officer cleared his throat. "We'll try to locate the family first. Whose property it was found on is a little questionable since your property line goes down to the road, and they were under the roadway."

"So do I get to keep it?" Kylie asked again.

The officer blushed. "If we don't locate family, there's a good chance of it, but we can't say for sure at this point."

"May I?" Kylie asked before reaching into the box.

"Be my guest," the coroner held out his hands in offering.

Kylie reached in and pulled out the locket on the thin chain. "This is just like the one we found in the tunnel to the garage," she reminded the chief.

"There's another?" the officer asked with interest.

Kylie nodded as she opened the locket. "Oh, this one is different." She tilted it towards Chief Lange to show him the tiny, jeweled poker chip inside.

"Is the outside identical?" the chief asked her.

Kylie closed it and nodded. "Yes." She looked at the officer. "Were they married?"

The officer shook his head. "Our preliminary investigation tells us the female, Phyllis Fairfield, was married to Henry Fairfield."

Kylie nodded, still looking at the locket. "And who were they?"

The officer shuffled some papers on the table in front of him. "Miss Fairfield was a member of the prominent Whitley family of Detroit."

"As in the Whitley Restaurant in the mansion?" Kylie asked, sounding impressed.

The officer looked at her. "You know it?"

She shrugged and blushed. "I'm a pastry chef. Restaurants are my thing. They have a maple-raspberry croissant bread pudding to die for there," she informed. She looked back at the locket. "So this woman that lived in that mansion died in my tunnel?"

"Well, she didn't live there after she got married," the officer informed.

Kylie looked at him. "But she wasn't married to this man she died in the tunnel with?"

"Nope," the officer confirmed.

"So who was the man?"

The officer reached into the box and pulled out the billfold. Slipping out the picture ID, he handed it to the cupcake-maker. "Paul Preston. He was a member of the Purple Gang of Detroit that owned and operated the club."

Kylie looked up at the officer. "So all of the rumors and stories about the gang owning it are true?"

He nodded. "Mr. Preston had disappeared off the radar of the Detroit police after a murder in broad daylight in the lobby of a prestigious Detroit hotel."

"So he came here," Kylie thought aloud.

"Apparently."

Kylie thumbed through the contents in the billfold until she came upon a photograph of a beautiful young woman with short, dark brown waves in her hair. Her skin was flawless, and her lipstick was dark. She studied the photograph before holding it up to the officer. "Do you know who this is?"

The officer plucked the photograph from her hand and turned it over to hold the back up to Kylie.

"Phyllis," Kylie mumbled aloud as she read the back of the photo. She took the photo back and looked intently at the image of the young heiress who had died in her tunnel before asking, "So why were they in the tunnel together if she was married to someone else?"

The officer shrugged. "We can only speculate. What I can tell you from my records search is that Mr. Preston mysteriously vanished the night of a raid on the club in 1930."

"1930?" Kylie whispered in awe.

He nodded before continuing. "Mrs. Fairfield was not reported missing until two days later."

Kylie furrowed her brow. "Why did it take two days for someone to notice she was missing?"

The officer shrugged. "As I said, all we can do is speculate. Maybe her husband was out of town. Maybe he conducted his own search before calling the authorities." His eyes moved back to the box of contents. "Maybe his wife was kidnapped."

Kylie shook her head. "There would be a ransom note and newspaper stories." She looked at the officer. "There weren't any of those things, were there?"

"Not that I found in my preliminary search."

Kylie rubbed the closed locket between two fingers. "Or they could have been running away together."

The officer rolled his eyes as he let out a breath of air and hoisted his belt of his pants higher. "Not likely her type would be cavorting around with a known felon."

"He had her photograph in his billfold," Kylie observed. "He knew her."

"Maybe he took out a hit on her, or maybe he admired her from afar," the officer offered.

Now Kylie looked at the coroner. "So what did they die from? Did the gangster shoot her?"

"Asphyxiation," he responded in a flat tone.

Kylie thought a moment. "So they suffocated when the dirt fell in on them?"

The coroner nodded.

"How horrible," Kylie mumbled, leaning back in her chair. Chief Lange put a hand over hers, and she gripped it sadly. "So we'll never know their story?"

The officer shrugged. "We've solved the ninety-year-old mystery of their disappearance. Seems like that's a pretty good story to me."

Kylie looked back to the coroner. "Were there photos taken of the scene?"

The coroner looked surprised. "They're gruesome. Not something a young lady would want to see."

Kylie let out an exasperated sigh. "Oh, come on, we've all seen skeletons before. How much could be left after ninety years?"

The coroner shrugged and pushed a file folder towards her. "More than you'd expect thanks to the damp walls."

Kylie opened the folder to find photographs of the skeletons in every stage of excavation, including the last. "They were holding hands," she noticed, holding up one of the photographs of the lovers that had been buried mid stride. She ran her fingertips over the photo before murmuring again, "Holding hands." She looked back to the coroner. "Is there anything else you can tell me about them?"

He puffed out his cheeks with air as he picked up the file and glanced at it again, shaking his head. "Nothing exciting. Twenty-eight-year-old male and a thirty-one-year-old female. Died of asphyxiation. Apparently he was a manager of the club, and she was some kind of heiress." He shrugged his shoulders indicating that was the end of the information.

Kylie rubbed the locket between her fingers. "And there's nothing else?"

He released his breath as he shook his head, flipping through a few pages before looking up at her. "Oh. And she was pregnant."

CHAPTER 32

"You shouldn't have that dog off its leash," a woman chastised Kylie.

"It's the Dog Beach," Kylie defended.

"It's a pit bull."

"She's a mix," Kylie defended.

"They're bred to kill with jaws that lock down and don't release," the woman informed Kylie as she scooped her cocker spaniel into her arms as if to protect it from the frolicking puppy.

"Actually, if you knew anything about pit bulls," Kylie heard a male voice behind her, "you would know that they were bred in Victorian times because they were such good family dogs."

"Hmph," the woman grunted as she turned and carried her dog away protectively.

Kylie turned and saw Chief Jason Lange standing behind her in shorts and a collared shirt. Cupcake romped up to her savior joyously.

"Hey, girl," he greeted her, bending down.

"Oh, so now you're an expert on pit bulls?" Kylie asked with her hands on her hips.

He shrugged as Cupcake put her large paws on his knees. "I Googled it."

Kylie blushed and relaxed. "Listen," she shrugged as she searched for the word, "thanks. That lady was not being very nice to Cupcake."

"Anything for my favorite victim," the chief responded without looking up as he scratched Cupcake's head. He finally scooped her up and stood. "So why isn't Cupcake wet?"

"She's afraid of the water," Kylie said sadly as she stepped over to give the dog a kiss.

"You missed."

She blushed and smiled again before rising onto her tiptoes

and planting a soft kiss on the chief's cheek as Cupcake pushed herself up to do the same.

"A kiss from my two best girls," the chief announced as he leaned over to kiss Kylie on the lips. He finished with a gentle tap of his nose against hers. "Now let's teach this poor dog how to swim."

"Kylie Sue!"

Kylie turned to see her Aunt Judy hobbling towards her from the small parking lot with a cane.

"Aunt Judy, where's your walker?"

The stocky woman made a brushing motion with her hand. "It's long gone. I'm on the road to recovery."

"That's great news!" Kylie held out her arms triumphantly.

"No, it's not," Judy countered as she paused to push her thick glasses back up on her nose.

"Wait up, Kitten," Sam Shepard called from the parking lot as he hobbled towards the Dog Beach, cane in hand.

"Because Sam's on the road to recovery too," Judy finished her statement.

"I'm right behind you, Sweet Cheeks," came his declaration as he hobbled along, attempting to catch up.

Judy reached Kylie and promptly slapped her on the arm.

"Ow!"

"If you ever meddle in my love life again, I swear, I'll – "

"I didn't meddle."

"You went delivering cupcakes where they weren't ordered," she hissed as she pointed an accusatory finger at her niece.

"I'm telling you, Judy," the chief interrupted, "I think you should just eat one of those Love Spell cupcakes, too. Then you'll be even."

"I don't want to be even with Sam," Judy continued to hiss. "Couldn't you have slipped it to Arnold Schwarzenegger or someone?"

"Well, he wasn't in town," Kylie defended herself.

"I'm almost there, Fabulous," Sam called from a few yards away.

Aunt Judy rolled her eyes. "Now he's recovering, and I can't get away from him."

"Maybe you weren't meant to," Kylie smiled as she turned and walked towards the water, the chief following with Cupcake in his arms.

"Don't walk away from me, young lady. You need to fix this."

"I think you'll be fine, Aunt Judy."

"I think you need a Hate Spell cupcake."

Kylie waded into the water in her shorts and turned back to her aunt. "Hate is a pretty strong word for someone you don't even like."

"Who don't ya like?" Sam asked as he reached within earshot of the conversation.

Judy tightened her lips before mumbling. "No one. I'm just suggesting a new cupcake flavor to Kylie."

"Mmm," he lifted his eyes to the sky in thought. "How about a lox and cream cheese flavored cupcake?"

Judy looked at him, appalled. "You want a fish-flavored cupcake?"

He shrugged. "Well, this is a town on the water. Maybe it will bring in some of the fishermen."

Judy rolled her eyes, and Sam leaned in and gave her a kiss on the cheek. "That's what I like about you, always helping out everyone else."

Judy let out a grunt, and Kylie and Chief Lange exchanged knowing glances.

"That's Aunt Judy," Kylie declared, "always thinking of everyone else." Hiding her grin, she pretended to look towards The

Point as Cupcake stepped timidly along the waterline.

"I'm starting to wonder about those Love Spell cupcakes," Chief Lange said as he waded in a few steps behind her.

Kylie mischievously smiled up at him. "Don't tell me you believe in legends and spells now, too."

He reached for her hand and turned her to him. "I wouldn't discount anything you came up with, Miss Cupcake."

Kylie squeezed his hand happily. "So I guess we've found the secret tunnels everyone has been whispering about for years, and Paul and Phyllis have finally been laid to rest." She shrugged her shoulders. "I guess everything is all wrapped up."

The chief smiled a knowing smile. "Oh, there are lots of other secrets to uncover in this small town."

Kylie's eyebrows raised. "Really? Like what?"

He shrugged noncommittally. "I can't tell you now, or you wouldn't have any reason to keep me around."

She batted his arm playfully. "Tell me!"

He looked up and rubbed his chin thoughtfully. "Yep. The more I think about it, the more I think you're going to need a local to fill you in on all of our small-town secrets."

Kylie mimicked his thoughtful motions. "Well, you do seem to come in pretty handy." She turned her eyes to his. "How much is this going to cost me in cupcakes?"

He shrugged as his arms moved to her waist and pulled her close. "We'll work something out."

Kylie's eyes moved to his lips. "Careful, I might slip in a Love Spell cupcake."

His lips lowered to hers and kissed her softly. "I don't think I need it."

EPILOGUE

"Willy, where are you?" Maddie called as she ran through the tall summer grass in her light blue cotton dress. She stopped and wrapped her white cardigan around herself as the breeze from the lake blew back her long, light brown locks. "I can't see you. Where are you?" Her eyes scanned the horizon.

Ahead of her, Willy rose from the tall grass where he had been sitting in their spot above the tunnel and waiting. "I'm over here," he shouted.

Maddie smiled and continued her run.

"I've been waiting for you," he announced once she was within earshot.

She wrapped her sixteen-year-old arms around his shoulders in greeting. "I knew you would."

He lifted and spun her around, holding her close for a long time. When she released her embrace, he ran his thumb over her soft cheek, pushing back a strand of hair blown out of place. "I was getting worried." He kissed her softly on the lips.

She smiled a dimpled smile at him. "I'm here now."

His eyes moved down to something shining on her chest. "You found your locket!"

Maddie's hand moved to it protectively. "Yes. A girl found it and gave it back to me."

He smiled his impish grin. "I'm glad you got back my collateral."

Two of her fingertips rubbed it as if it were magic. "I'll never take it off again."

He dropped his hand to grip hers. "Are you ready to go?"

Her eyes scrunched as she smiled at him and nodded. "I'm ready."

Hand in hand, the two young lovers walked down the hillside, past the tunnel entrance, and across the field of tall grass towards the bright blue waters of the bay, glimmering in the sunlight.

Behind them, at the entrance to the tunnel, stood Paul Preston in his white dinner jacket and black bowtie. His arms were wrapped protectively around the abdomen of Phyllis, revealing a small bulge in her waistline. Still in her white dinner dress, she pressed her back to him, her hands wrapped around his.

Paul leaned down and kissed her cheek as she tilted her head happily up to receive it. "I think I've changed my mind," she mused as she watched the two young lovers walking towards the bright blue bay.

"About what?" he asked.

"Maybe I do believe in love."

He smiled and snuggled his cheek to hers. "They say it's never too late." He kissed her cheek softly again before giving her a squeeze of dismissal. "Shall we go?"

She gave his hands a squeeze in return and nodded. "It took a long time, but I guess our story is finally over here."

Paul looked towards the bay. "But it's just beginning over there." He stepped to her side and took her hand. "I told you I'd have forever with you."

She gripped his hand as she looked ahead and rested her free hand on her abdomen. "With us," she corrected. "You'll have forever with us."

"Even better," he agreed, looking at her fondly. "Shall we go?"

Hand in hand, the notorious gangster and the heiress followed Maddie and Willy away from the tunnel and towards the glimmering blue water of the bay.

THE END

A NOTE FROM THE AUTHOR

Thank you for reading this story. I hope you enjoyed reading it as much as I enjoyed writing it. If you enjoyed it, please feel free to leave a rating or review at www.Amazon.com.

As a graduate of Harbor Springs High School, I first heard about the secret tunnels when I was in college. It was something that has always stayed in the back of my mind until the opportunity came along to write this story. I worked closely with local historian Richard Wiles so that I could get the details correct. He sent me photographs, diagrams, and countless articles that helped me put this story together. I'd like to extend a special thank you to him.

Maybe the secret of the tunnels and all of the lives that were changed by Club Manitou will forever haunt our small town's history. Maybe I've passed along enough information to give you closure. Maybe you'll never be satisfied until you find a tunnel yourself. Whatever the outcome, I hope I piqued your interest. I hope to have another Harbor Secret book out in late 2016.

Other books by Kristie Dickinson:

Nine Days In Greece

Risking The Nine Days

Before The Nine Days

Nine Days Ever After

The Back of his Mind – a short story

You can find my web site at www.Kdickinson.Homestead.com. At www.daterella.wordpress.com, my blog, I share some of my thoughts on love, dating, and relationships. If you would like to personally contact me, you can reach me at Dickinson.Kristie@gmail.com.

Made in the USA
Lexington, KY
18 September 2016